RAVENOUS

K.M. SCOTT

RAVENOUS

Cash March has everything going for him. With stunning good looks and a sharp mind, he's set to graduate from law school in just a few months. His future looks bright.

The son of Cassian and Olivia will be the first lawyer in the family. Talk about proud.

Except Cash is hiding something, and if that secret is found out, he may lose everything, including his future.

Savannah Gardener knows far too much about loss. A widow before her twenty-seventh birthday, she longs for the life she thought was hers before fate shattered her dreams.

She has everything a woman could want, except love. All her money can't buy that. Maybe it can help her find something to make her smile with a sexy man who's looking for happiness too, though.

But will Cash's secrets ruin any chance for them when the truth is finally revealed?

ISBN: 978-1-955335-02-7

UP AT THE HOUSE, MY MOTHER AND GRANDMOTHER talk about all the parties they need to plan for the next year like it's the central focus of their lives. No doubt, my family knows how to have a good time. It's a March tradition. If there's something to be celebrated, we get together and do it up big. Even when there's only a handful of us hanging out, we know how to party.

I just wish my mother would focus on someone other than me and what's happening in my life when it comes to her event planning.

Turning to look at my younger brother relaxing in the beach chair next to me, his eyes closed and his face placid like nothing in the world could even come close to bothering him, I say, "Do you hear Mom and

Grandma up there? I think they've been talking about that same subject for the past hour."

Alex slowly opens his eyes and turns his head toward me. "What subject? I'm not listening to them. Some beers, probably too much sun, and swimming for a couple hours this afternoon wiped me out. I think I fell asleep there for a while. What are they talking about?"

Oh, to be my brother and have the attitude toward life he has. I don't know where he got it from since my mother and father are both Type A people, but Alex is nothing like the three of us. He looks at the world as nothing but a good time to be had, and whatever that involves, whether it be food, drink, sex, or smoke, he's happy to simply enjoy it all.

"Mom's cataloguing the parties we all need to hold, and Grandma is making them grow exponentially bigger, like she always does. At any moment, Dad's going to chime in with something and before you know it, we'll be hanging out here eating and drinking every weekend until next Fourth of July."

With a shrug, Alex lets out a sigh. "You've been in this family long enough that I'd think you'd know what they're all about. I don't see why you'd have a problem with any of what they're talking about. You get to be the star at one of their parties next year when you graduate. All the food and drink you and everyone you've ever met in life right here to celebrate you finishing law school."

My mind flashes back to when Alex graduated from culinary school. So much food. So many people.

Talk about a lost weekend. That party will go down in the annals of March celebrations, for sure.

But I'm not my brother, and the thought of having to mix and mingle with all sorts of guests here only because my parents are so proud they invite every damn soul they've ever spoken to makes me cringe.

"It's not like I discovered a cure for cancer or anything," I mumble under my breath.

Next to me on my left sits Liam, who I know has been listening to my mother all this time. I glance over at him and see him smirk. Like with most things, he says little but the look on his face tells you he has an opinion on whatever's going on.

"Well, you might as well say it. It's written all over your face," I say.

He shakes his head and laughs. "What? You just seem awfully touchy about having a party thrown in your honor."

"It's not that."

Liam sits up straight in his chair and leans over to grab his drink. "Then what is it? You know how our parents get. Every one of us got the full party treatment for every birthday and graduation. I'm not sure why this one is bothering you."

Of course, he doesn't understand. Nobody does. I don't talk to anyone in our family about what my life's been like since I moved away to go to law school.

I wave away anything I might want to say, knowing that the more I complain, the more interested my brother and cousin will be in my life. That's the last thing I need. I love my family, but I don't love them in my business.

"It's probably too much sun, like Alex said. I guess I'm getting cranky."

Eager to change the subject, I ask him about his life, happy to have the focus move to him. "So why aren't you off doing your job with that music star instead of here? I thought your job with her started already?"

Liam twists his expression into a scowl. "It got postponed because she checked into rehab. For the next three months, I get to do all the sitting on the beach and drinking I want, I guess."

I know him well enough that the last thing he wants to do is lounge out for that long. Liam may choose to say very little at times, but he's more like me and my Type A personality than like my brother. Alex would love to just sit at the edge of the water and look out toward the horizon for days on end. As long as he could indulge in whatever desires arose in him, he'd be as happy as a clam.

"You can't take any other security jobs?"

Shaking his head, Liam gives me another grimace. "She's gone for just long enough that any assignments are impossible. If she could hang out at that cushy place for even four months, then I could take something to fill the time before I start with her, but three months doesn't work. I mean, I can do some one day jobs, but there's not much in those."

On my right, Alex says, "Must be nice to just be able to sit around for months on end. When I grow up,

I think I want to be you, Liam. Or Cash here. But instead, I get to be me."

Liam and I laugh at my brother's faux woe is me routine. "You love what you do, Alex," I say, knowing how much his job means to him.

"Yeah. Why are you acting like doing your job isn't the thing you love the most in life?" Liam asks with a chuckle.

Alex sits up and leans over to look at the two of us. With a sly smile, he nods. "I do, but I wouldn't be against hanging out for a few months."

"Trust me," Liam says in his serious voice. "You don't want to be me or Cash. If you want to be anyone, it's Wilder. Now there's a guy who's living his best life."

I give my brother a quick glance of recognition at the hint of sarcasm in Liam's voice. Closer to Wilder than any of the rest of us in the family, except for Kane and Abbi, he says little about his adopted brother, but when he does talk about him, what he says always seems to be tinged with something dark, like if he ever did decide to really get chatty about Wilder, he'd have something pretty damn big to say.

But while I never venture into those waters with my cousin, Alex has no issues with giving his opinion about Wilder. "Oh yeah? Has he moved on from busting up my kitchen to bigger and better things?"

No missing the contempt there.

"I don't know," Liam says as he sits back in his chair and takes a drink of his beer. "We aren't exactly close these days. I'm usually working, so I don't see him much."

"I noticed he isn't here today," I say as I look around for any sign of him.

Neither Liam nor Alex say anything to that, even though I have a sense my brother would love to respond. That he doesn't is only because he likes Liam.

"You three have been down here all afternoon. Are you avoiding us up at the house?"

I turn around to see my father walking toward where we sit. Dressed in his usual dress pants and a blue golf shirt, Cassian March looks like the quintessential businessman. Every day of my life, my father has looked like this. I admire him for that, though. He cares about what he looks like, even after being married to my mother for all these years. He never let himself go or stopped caring like a lot of guys do once they settle down.

He's the picture of success, and he's proud of it.

"We can hear Mom down here talking about all the parties coming up," I say, forcing a smile. "I figured I'd stay out of the way of all that. I can't say why these two flanking me have grown roots, though."

Alex and Liam laugh at my attempt to throw them under the bus. "This is where I always camp out at these things, so no need to wonder about me," Alex says.

"I'm sulking about my job situation, so you don't want me up there with you guys," Liam says quietly.

"I heard about your client's unfortunate turn of

events," my father says, nodding his head like he's sympathetic.

Only Cassian March could refer to someone getting in trouble with drugs and forced to go to rehab by the court as an unfortunate turn of events and sound sincere.

"Yeah, well, I'm sulking about it with your sons today, Cassian."

My father gives him another nod and turns his attention to me. "As for your mother and her party planning, she's got the event of the season coming up with your graduation party. It's not every day that a person graduates from law school, so she's pulling out all the stops."

"I heard. It's really not such a big deal, Dad. I mean, I appreciate all she's doing, but it's just like when I graduated from college."

All my father hears in that is some fake humility and not my real desire for no big party. "Are you kidding? You're going to be the first lawyer in the family, Cash. You have no idea how much Stefan, Kane, and I could have used a lawyer who was related to us all those times we got into scrapes."

My father, the king of euphemisms. Unfortunate turn of events. Scrapes. What he so lightly terms scrapes were more than once when each of them, my father and my two uncles, were looking at real jail time. The businessman in his golf shirt standing in front of me wasn't always the upstanding citizen he is today.

And my uncles? They were even worse.

Liam laughs at that and says, "I've heard my father say the amount you three used to pay in legal bills for Stefan alone used to make him want to tear his hair out."

Throwing his head back, my father lets out a belly laugh at that memory. "Your uncle did have a way of keeping this town's lawyers in business. That guy you see now isn't the one Kane and I had to work with. You get the grown up version of your uncle. We got the OG Stefan."

"Too bad Cade isn't here. He loves hearing about his father back in the day," Alex says, now interested in the conversation.

"It's better he isn't. It only gives him more ammunition for those fights he and my brother have over the club. Shay said he and Hailey had to leave early today. So much for gang of five like it's always been."

"Yeah. We single guys have to fly solo now," Alex says with a sigh.

Before my father can say another word, my mother walks up behind me and tousles my hair. "You should know your grandmother and I are planning the party to end all parties for when you graduate, Cassian March IV."

I always know she's serious when she uses my full name and includes the fourth. She makes me sound like I'm some king waiting in the wings for the third to give up his throne.

Tilting my head back, I look up at her and force a smile. "You really don't have to do that, Mom. I know you guys are proud and everything, but you don't have to make a big deal. Honest."

Thankfully, my grandmother announcing that Wilder has shown up deflects my parents' attention from me and their celebration plans. My mother quickly kisses the top of my head and then my brother's before she and my father walk back up to the porch to welcome our cousin. Like always, it reeks of overcompensation, as if Wilder requires so much reassurance that everyone loves him that all attention must be paid to him.

On a normal day, it would grate on my nerves, but today, I'm thankful for him being a distraction.

Leaning over toward Alex, I say in a low voice, "I'll even take having to deal with Wilder if it means it takes the focus off of me for a little while."

For one of the few times I can remember, my brother looks at me with complete seriousness in his eyes. "You're a big deal, Cash. Mom and Dad are prouder than I've ever seen them. You can't blame them. This is huge."

"Is being a lawyer that important? It's not more impressive than your being a chef."

A smile brightens his dark brown eyes. "Yes, it is. If you're thinking I'm bothered by all of this attention on you, don't. I'm fine with it. You deserve it, Cash. Graduating from law school is a big fucking deal."

"Not really. It's just school. I read the books and took the tests. Nothing special."

He studies my face for a long moment before asking, "Why do you sound so unhappy? You've wanted to be a lawyer since you were old enough to answer the question 'What do you want to be when you grow up?' Your answer has never changed. You always said you wanted to be a lawyer. You're almost there. You got the brass ring. Enjoy it."

Under my breath, I repeat those words, "Enjoy it."

Alex points his finger toward my face. "See, that's what your problem is. Type A's like you don't know how to enjoy what you've earned. Take it from someone who definitely knows how to enjoy things. This is something you savor. As for Mom and Dad, they're just trying to enjoy your success in their own way. Just go with it and have fun. You earned it."

I hear my grandmother mention the graduation party and know my reprieve courtesy of Wilder's arrival is already over. So much for that short-lived chance to not deal with the reality of next spring.

CHAPTER TWO

ash

"FIVE HUNDRED SAYS THE DOLPHINS DON'T MAKE the playoffs this year," Damon says, pointing his right hand and the beer bottle in it toward the TV. "I swear to God they have an allergy to fucking winning."

A diehard Miami fan, he says things like this before every season and every game. Just to bust his balls, I say, "You know, has it ever occurred to you that you jinx them when you say things like that? And betting on them to not make the playoffs seems like you're just begging for them to fail."

He lifts the bottle to his mouth and takes a drink before rolling his eyes. "You sound like that girl I was seeing a while back. She was always going on about me putting negativity into the universe. Are you on that bullshit now?"

I can't help but laugh at how touchy he gets whenever he's talking about his team. Anything else, Damon's as cool as a cucumber. He's a lot like my brother in that way. But get him talking about football and he becomes unglued.

"No. I just thought I'd put it out there. Maybe you should think positively about them. It couldn't hurt. I think it's the only part of your life you're not sure is going to succeed beyond your wildest dreams. You know that?"

A look of utter disgust comes over his face. "That's because I'm not in control of what they do every Sunday. If I was, they'd have a better defensive line, for Christ's sake, and they'd draft a decent quarterback and stop trying to make do with the fucking castoffs from other teams. They run that team like it's a pig on fucking stilts."

The image of that fills my mind, and I throw my head back and laugh. "So much for positive thoughts, huh? I guess I should be thankful you don't talk like this about our business."

After taking another gulp of beer, he sets his bottle down on the table in front of him. "Our business is run like a goddamned business should be. They run that team like it's some half-hearted effort nobody gives a shit about."

I'd love to change the subject, but all I can think about is my family and their need to throw the biggest party the city of Tampa has ever seen, and that's including when they won the damn Super Bowl. I think I need to skip going to my grandmother's for a few trips.

Damon breaks into my thoughts with something about a class we took in our first year of law school. I don't hear every word he says, though, so I just shake my head.

"What? Sorry, I was off in space there."

"I said, I saw Justin Connor over the weekend. Remember, he was in Trusts and Estates with us? You should hear him now. I swear to God, man, he's like everything I have nightmares about. All he could talk about was how he's all in on taking advantage of the millions of boomers who are going to need estate planning."

Simply hearing that makes my head hurt. Estate planning? Fucking boring.

"I can't believe we thought we wanted to do that with our lives."

Damon nods in agreement and gets up out of his leather recliner. "No kidding. Jesus, it was like standing there listening to someone from another planet, Cash. You want another beer?"

Quickly, I finish the last few mouthfuls and hand him my empty. "Yeah, one more before I go."

As he walks into the kitchen, he tosses the bottles into the garbage and yells out to me, "And you should have seen him. He looked like someone had just handed him the magic fucking ticket to success. All I could do was stand there and hope someone hot would walk by so I could at least have something to think about while I was trapped listening to him."

When he returns, he hands me my fresh beer.

"That's the last time I do Candy a favor and go to her housewarming thing. What the hell is that anyway? Hey, here's my new place. Bring me gifts and I'll feed you while you're stuck listening to boring as fuck people talk about everything but the new place!"

More people who are all about the party. Not that Damon and I don't enjoy a good time. We just have other goals than being stuck in a room with people we don't give a shit about.

"What's her new house look like?" I ask, happy I had to beg off to go to my family's get-together this weekend.

Damon shrugs and sits down in his recliner he loves. "Same as any other house in Gainesville. I got the hell out of there as early as possible after giving her a blender and then getting trapped talking to Estate Planning Justin."

Guess I didn't miss much.

"You know, I'd want to kill myself every morning if I had to do that shit Justin's so jacked up about. I've always been more of an entrepreneur, myself," Damon says proudly before taking a big drink of beer.

"Same here," I say, lifting my bottle in a silent toast to the two of us conquering our little part of the business world so successfully in the past couple years.

"So how were things while I was back at the homestead?" I ask.

"Same as always. You should never doubt how many lonely women there are around here, and how many guys need money more than love."

"Don't we all?" I say with a chuckle.

Truer words have never been spoken. Money can't buy you love, but it can buy you everything else, and then you can deal with love.

"Thank God for Bitcoin, though," I say, seriously wondering how the hell anyone ran a business like ours before cryptocurrencies. "Can you imagine how hard it would be if we had to deal with credit cards or checks?"

With a hard eye roll, Damon sneers at the very words. "Talk about shit I'm not going to do. Checks? I think my grandmother is the only person who writes those anymore. Every year for my birthday, she sends me twenty dollars. It's nice, but I keep telling her to just keep it. She doesn't listen, though."

"I wouldn't touch any of it with credit cards or checks. Maybe with cash, but damn, that sounds risky as hell," I comment, thinking out loud.

"Sounds dirty as fuck. Do you know how filthy dollar bills are? I'm surprised we didn't die off as a species with all the disgusting germs those things carry on them."

While he goes off on some show he watched about the bubonic plague being found on a hundred dollar bill somewhere out in the southwest, I mentally go through how many times I touched food or parts of my body that day after paying for a meal on the way home. Jesus, paper money is disgusting. I think I need a shower.

Somewhere in the midst of my cringing over touching money in the past twelve hours, Damon switches gears and starts talking about some article he read recently. He's always watching something or reading something in order to make the business more profitable. I can appreciate that in a partner, which makes his mood swings easier to deal with.

"I read that September weddings are becoming more popular. This article said they're going to surpass June weddings as the most popular time of the year to get married."

"Here in Florida? September is prime time for hurricanes," I say, silently wondering why people would spend thousands of dollars just to have everything ruined by some storm.

"I didn't say people getting married are the smartest tools in the shed, man. I just said that's what I read. I don't know if it was geographically centered," he says with a laugh.

"Well, good luck to them. Hope it doesn't all blow away," I joke.

Damon waves his arm through the air. "Whatever. All I'm saying is shit's about to get busy. Do you think we have enough guys?"

I quickly run through the roster of people we have working for us that I can rely on if things start to get crazy. I'm not sure we have enough, but I haven't had time to find new guys lately.

"We should be good, but if it gets wild, they might have to double up on assignments."

"Just as long as I don't have to take any of the jobs. Ashley is hard enough to deal with normally. She finds out I'm even out with some woman in a car, forget about anything else, and my life will go from happy to goddamned nightmare in like two point five seconds."

I laugh, but he's actually underestimating how his girlfriend would react if she saw him out with someone else. Ashley personifies the emotion of jealousy. She's practically green from it.

Not that Damon makes it easy on her to think he's not cheating every night of the week. I bet in the past seven days, he hasn't called her five times. It's the reason she routinely shows up here like some fucking SEAL team commando ready to break down the door whenever I'm over. I'm surprised she hasn't shown up already tonight, but maybe he called her today.

If not, she'll be banging on the door screaming about how he has some nerve doing her wrong and she knows all about what he's up to. She has no idea. Nobody does.

Except me, of course.

I finish up my beer and stand up to toss it into the kitchen garbage. It misses, bouncing off the side of the refrigerator and onto the floor before skidding into the island.

"Nice job, Cash. Don't quit your day job for that gig in the NBA, man," Damon teases.

"I'm not tall enough. Six three in the NBA is practically a garden gnome," I joke as I pick up my bottle and place it into the garbage can this time.

As I turn to say goodbye on my way out, my phone vibrates in my pocket. Fishing it out, I look at the screen to see the only name I don't want to deal with tonight.

"Let me guess. By the look on your face, I'm willing to bet it's Emily," Damon says as I stuff my phone back into my pocket without reading her message.

I grunt out something that sounds like yes mixed with fuck. That's how much I don't want to deal with her now. Or anytime, for that matter.

"She's back to texting you?"

"Never really stopped. I just don't answer most of them."

"That's your problem right there, man. You answer some of them. That gives her hope. You're just fucking cruel, Cash. You keep stringing her along. You're going to get shit for it in the end. You need to deal with it like a Band-Aid. Rip it off, no matter how much it hurts."

"I already did the rip it off thing. We broke up months ago. And I don't think telling someone to stop texting is stringing along. She just won't give up."

With a shit-eating grin, he says, "She wants you to be her permanent escort."

If there's a more disgusting idea than that, I can't think of it at the moment. "No, thanks."

"I'm telling you, Cash. Rip that Band-Aid off and make it permanent, or you're going to suffer. Mark my words on that."

"See you later. Come by my place on Wednesday, earlier if anything comes up."

Damon laughs at the very mention of anything coming up in our business. "We run a finely tuned, well-oiled machine here, Cash. Nothing ever comes up, and that's how I like it. But I'll stop over anyway because I think Ashley has some museum thing she has going on that night. Definitely don't want to be roped into that. You should take lessons from me when it comes to women. Keep them at arm's length until you want something, and then you pull them in close. Thanks for coming to my TED talk."

I turn to leave and wave my hand as I roll my eyes. The last person in the world I want to take advice about women from is Damon. Business? Sure. Women? Hell, no.

TOSSING MY KEYS ON THE HALLWAY TABLE, I HEAD into my living room to relax. After dealing with my family and business with Damon, I need to close my eyes and push the world away for a few minutes. My phone vibrates again, the second time since I left Damon's twenty minutes ago, but I don't even bother to look at who it could be.

I already know. Emily. She's the only person in my life who texts like some obsessive teenager on a self-destructive emotional spiral.

After the third time, I open my eyes, disgusted I haven't convinced her to go away with my non-answers. I take my phone out of my pocket and see I was right. Four texts in a half hour. Unless the house is burning the fuck down, she shouldn't be messaging me like this, and if it is on fire, call the goddamned fire department and leave me alone.

I turn the phone off and pitch it to the end of the

sofa. Maybe I should let it get lost in the cushions for a few days. It's not like that could hurt business since it's not the phone I use for that.

Even in my disgust, I look around and can't help but think I've done pretty damn well for myself in the past couple years. The finest furniture, seventy-five inch TV, the best that money can buy in everything.

As I glance at all the things I've bought, even as I know it's a drop in the bucket compared to what I have in my bank accounts, I notice my books from my first year in law school sitting on the bookcase. When was the last time I opened any of them up?

I can't believe I even kept those books.

That was a life I never knew I hated until Damon and I started our business. Classes like that one we met Justin Connor in made me realize the last thing I wanted to do was handle estate planning or anything else involving the law. Back then, I saw no way out. I was in law school, and I'd graduate in three years and take the bar.

My future was set in stone.

Until that one weekend when Mari, a girl in one of our classes desperately needed a date for her sister's wedding after her asshole boyfriend broke up with her two nights before the big day. She told Damon her tale of woe, and he suggested I take her since I had been complaining about life being all school and no play.

So I did, and now I can't remember if I had a good time or bad. All I remember is Mari giving us two hundred bucks and saying we saved her life. Since I didn't sleep with her, I wasn't sure what I'd done to deserve anything after eating some great food and enjoying an open bar at the wedding reception for three hours, but she told us she knew at least half a dozen women just like her who needed guys to help them out like I helped her.

They didn't want full-time relationships. They wanted someone to take them to family obligations and make them look good.

And so our business was born.

At first, it was just for extra money, but when we made half a million in the first year, we knew we could walk away from law school since neither one of us gave a damn about becoming lawyers anyway.

From that day on, life has been great. I only have one problem.

How am I going to break it to my parents that there's no reason for some big party next spring because there's nothing to celebrate?

CHAPTER THREE

avannah

THE WEDDING INVITATION SITS ON THE TABLE IN front of me in all its very expensive parchment glory. It sat unopened until this morning, not that I had to read the words printed on the paper to know what it was.

My oldest sibling, my brother Spencer, is set to get married this Saturday to his longtime girlfriend Daria. I'm not close to my brother, but that doesn't matter. Attending this wedding is mandatory, and no excuse will suffice.

Not even the one I've used for the past two years. It seems the reason of not wanting to be around people because you're still in mourning for your dead husband has reached its expiration date.

Maybe if it was up to my father I could beg off, but

since he's simply along for the ride when it comes to family events like this, I knew I'd have to attend. My mother and my older sister Cecile would make sure of it, even if they had to drag me from this house kicking and screaming. Two of a kind, they believe there's an expiration date on mourning, and according to them, I reached it about a year back.

If I'm being honest, I haven't actually been in mourning for all that time. Carson wouldn't want me to be holed up inside this big house, roaming its cavernous hallways all alone day after day. My husband would want me to go on living, and in many ways, I've done that because I know he wouldn't expect me to shrivel up and die because he's gone.

He always hated funerals. Of all the things he loathed about being who he was, the worst was attending funerals. He said it made him feel old and being fifty felt old enough. He didn't need to attend a steady parade of death events to drive home just how much life he didn't have left.

Many people thought that's why he married someone half his age. Just twenty-five when I said yes to his proposal, I didn't see him as an old man. He was just Carson Gardener, the gorgeous and powerful owner of Sterling Hotels to me. He didn't act like an old person either. He acted like a man in love, so age didn't matter.

Not his and not mine. At least not to us.

I knew when I married him that we'd never get to celebrate a golden anniversary, and not simply because that would put him at one hundred years old if we reached that milestone. Carson never had that much time left, and he knew it. So did I. I went into our marriage with my eyes wide open.

He warned me people would think horrible things, like I married him just to wait out his death. Or that he finally settled down after dating all those beautiful women around the world, the operative word being settled.

Settled for me.

"Don't listen to any of it, Savannah," he always said. "I married you because I wanted the last years of my life to be sweet and happy. You're the only person who's ever given me those two most important qualities to my world. Let them talk. You'll be an obscenely wealthy woman when I'm gone anyway, so it will be more jealousy than anything else."

And when he died right after my twenty-sixth birthday, that's exactly what happened. People did talk. They said nasty things about me being a gold digger. Some claimed Carson must have suffered from early senility and didn't know what he was doing when he married such a young woman and then left her everything. Others went so far as to say I probably killed him to get everything since they couldn't imagine someone so young would ever want to spend any time around a man twice her age.

None of that was true. It didn't matter, though. The gossip in all the social circles that had once welcomed the two of us with open arms made seeing any of the people Carson believed were his friends impossible. Media stalked me from the moment his death was announced, sure my trips to the store or to my family would reveal the truth—that I had a lover the entire time and now I would live happily ever after with him, the young stud assumed to be hiding in the shadows just waiting for my husband to keel over dead.

But that wasn't true either.

I had no one but my family, and even among them I felt alone. Only my younger sister Cheyenne understood the pain I was going through. My brother Spencer, ten years older and never close with me, visited once and then disappeared from my life. Not that I entirely blame him. We weren't exactly bosom buddies before my husband's death. Ten years is a span of time the two of us could never bridge, and tragedy wasn't going to change that fact.

My older sister Cecile never liked Carson, so it was no surprise that his death didn't bring out any warm feelings in her. I'm not even sure she possesses warmth inside her. Seven years older than me, she has always been much like Spencer.

Too separated from me in age to be much of a sister.

So she's always behaved more like an overseer for Cheyenne and me, swooping in when we're about to do something to warn us how terrible the results will likely be and standing in judgment when those results come anywhere close to what she predicted. Cheyenne hates her and never lets a chance go by to tell her exactly how much. I mostly think of her as someone who wishes she'd smothered me at birth, and ever since then, she's done all she can to achieve that same result figuratively, if not literally.

Is it any wonder I've dreaded attending this wedding?

I'm not in mourning anymore, though, so I don't have a choice. At least not the kind of mourning that's acceptable to most of my family.

Lifting the invitation up, I run the pad of my thumb over the paper. It reminds me of the wedding invitations I picked out just a few years ago. My prospective sister-in-law made a point to mention to me back then that she loved how luxurious mine felt in her hand when she took it out of the envelope. Things like that make an impression on Daria, so I'm not surprised she used the information I gave her about where I'd had our invitations made when Carson and I returned from our honeymoon.

My mind wanders back to those two weeks in Bali we spent with practically no one else around, except for the maid who came in once a day to clean and change the sheets and the waiters who brought us our room service. We only left the villa to venture out onto the beach and take a swim every few hours before hurrying back to bed.

I shake my head to make that memory disappear. This is why I didn't want to have anything to do with my brother's wedding. All it does is bring back all those thoughts and feelings I've tried so hard to push to the back of my mind.

How am I ever supposed to get on with my life like Carson wanted me to and everyone else says I should when all I can do is remember how much I loved my life back then? How am I to move on from something so wonderful?

"Savannah! Where are you?" my sister Cheyenne yells at the top of her lungs.

The house repeats her question, echoing her booming voice in the emptiness. "I'm here in the living room," I call back, nowhere as loud as her but the house will do its job to amplify my answer.

She marches down the hallway, her flip flops smacking off the white marble tile floor. Cheyenne used to joke when we first moved into this home right after we got married that her fifteen dollar flip flops on floors that cost thousands of dollars might be considered some kind of crime in the circles Carson and I traveled in.

I found out they discriminate far worse than that. By now, my sister's cheap flip flops would be the least of my supposed crimes to all those people.

"I'm here, so let the party start!" she announces with a big smile that shows off the fantastic result of years of her wearing braces on her teeth.

My sister never fails to amaze me with how hard she tries to make me see there's still a reason to keep living. When the rest of my family gave up on me as a hopeless, lost cause last year, Cheyenne was the one who showed up every day after work.

A kindergarten teacher, she's wickedly funny, a trait that's unfortunately wasted on five year olds and their helicopter parents. She's also beautiful, but not in the traditional sense of the word. Never a slave to her weight, she happily keeps a few extra pounds on her that she says makes sure she always keeps it real.

"We're partying today?" I ask as she sets down her enormous pink purse big enough to stow one of her students in. "I didn't realize we had that on the schedule. I just thought this was a regular Cheyenne visit."

She runs her hands through her shoulder length light brown hair I think has some new blond highlights in it and sits down hard in the chair next to me. "Every day is a party, Savannah. You know, I promised Carson I'd never let you forget that. I think I might be falling down on the job by the looks of you."

Instantly losing my focus on her hair and how I intended on asking her what she had done, I look down at the pale pink sundress I'm wearing and then back up at her. "What's wrong with the way I look? This dress is one of my favorites."

Cheyenne levels her gaze hard on my face and scowls. "I'm not talking about the dress. You always look incredible. I'm talking about everything from the neck up. You look miserable. What's up? Because that is not a party face."

I lift the invitation from the table and turn it around to show it to her. "I'm dreading this weekend. If I look miserable, that's the cause."

"Yeah, me too. Spencer always acts like he's my weird old uncle instead of my only brother. I can see him right in the middle of the wedding toast marching right over to us at the lame single table he and Daria stuck us at and giving us a lecture on why our dresses are too low cut or how we should wear less makeup. Thank God there's going to be alcohol at this shindig or I'd be a no-show."

The way she describes our older brother makes me laugh, mostly because it sounds exactly like how he behaves around the two of us. Spencer is the finest example of old before his time I've ever seen in my life.

"Let's hope Daria's family keeps him busy. Have you met her mother and father? I'm convinced they think Spencer has some secret stash of gold hidden somewhere by the way they treat him," I say, remembering the few times I've been around them and saw how they acted like my brother is a god or something equally as impressive.

Cheyenne's eyes light up at my description of Daria's parents. "No, I haven't. I've never had the pleasure. See what I did there? I made sure to say that like a Marchand would because you know Mom and Cecile are going to be riding me from the moment I walk into that reception if I don't act appropriately."

I love how she pokes fun at how stuffy and fake my mother and sister behave whenever they're at one of these events. "Dahling, you're a Marchand. You must act accordingly or the peasants will think you belong with them," I say with a giggle.

"They're such frauds. You alone have ten times their money, but you don't act like that. And you were a Marchand before you became a Gardener, so you should be up to your ears in stuffiness."

Waving away that idea, I say to her what Carson used to say to me. "You can have all the money in the world, but if you aren't comfortable in your own skin, it doesn't matter."

She points at me and smiles. "See? That right there is why your husband was so cool. He had a bajillion dollars and still could hang out and be cool."

"He definitely could. You two sitting around the pool and doing tequila shots proved that."

For the first time, Cheyenne's bubbly personality seems to fade just a tiny bit. "Yeah, that was fun. He spoiled me with the good tequila too, you know that? Now when I go out for drinks and guys order the cheap stuff, I turn all snobby like Mom."

"I miss those days with you in the carriage house and Carson and me up here in this house. He'd always ask as soon as he got home if we were going to have a pool night. He loved hanging out with you and me."

My sister and I fall into silence as the memory of those times flashes through my mind. Carson and I didn't get to have happiness for long, but what we did have was wonderful.

Will I ever find that again? After two years of being alone, I've begun to doubt I'll get to be happy like I was then a second time in this life.

Maybe all the happiness I was supposed to have already happened.

CHAPTER FOUR

*S*avannah

CHEYENNE GIVES MY HAND A SYMPATHETIC SQUEEZE and smiles as tears fill my eyes. "Carson knew how to have a good time because he wasn't some old fuddy-duddy. He was the perfect mixture of serious guy at the office and fun guy at the pool. I hope I find someone like him someday, instead of the total toolbags I keep meeting."

Much happier to focus on my sister's inability to meet anyone good than my blissful past, I wipe the tear under my eye and ask, "Still no one you like?"

Raising her hands in front of her, she shakes her head in disgust. "I've given up. I'm convinced I'm never going to meet anyone decent, so I'm going it alone. If I need a guy on my arm for something like this thing this weekend, I'll just get a temporary boyfriend."

"Temporary boyfriend? What's that?" I ask, instantly intrigued since if my sister is touting this as a great idea, it's worth a listen.

"Exactly what it sounds like. A temporary man for a temporary need."

Those words filter through my brain, but I'm still not understanding. "All I'm hearing is gigolo, Cheyenne. Is that what you're talking about?"

She bursts into laughter, throwing her head back. "No, but I think that might be my new favorite word, thank you very much. Gigolo. Oh, yeah. That's the word for this weekend. Who's the man you're with, Cheyenne? Oh, this is just my gigolo. Cheyenne, your boyfriend dances so well. That's because he's a gigolo. I love it! Mom and Cecile will have a fit, and I'm pretty sure Spencer will faint dead away in horror. Too bad about that honeymoon, Daria."

"Are you saying you hired someone to go with you to this wedding?" I ask, getting more eager by the second to hear what she actually means about this temporary boyfriend concept of hers.

"Yeah! It's the perfect answer to those of us single girls who get stuck attending these ridiculous family things. The guy goes as your date, and no one is the wiser. He gets paid, you don't have to deal with the hundreds of questions all centered on when you're going to finally find someone so you don't end up some lonely spinster, as if that's anything any woman really cares about in the twenty-first century, and everyone goes home happy."

"How do you do it? What if someone like Aunt Grace asks him a question he doesn't know the answer to? Won't it be obvious you two aren't really together?"

None of this seems to concern my sister. "No, because we're newly dating. That's what everyone will think. They'll be impressed I'm with anyone at all since I usually go to these family events solo. The guy is basically just a blocker for you so if anyone wants to bother you, they have to deal with you and your boyfriend. They promise he's charming, knows how to act in whatever setting you tell them you need him for, and perfectly upstanding looking so your relatives don't think you've started dating a serial killer. It's perfect!"

It would be nice to be left alone at this wedding instead of having everyone hover over me like I'm some broken china doll no one knows how to fix. Last Christmas at my parents' house convinced me they're never going to stop seeing me as Savannah, wife of that man who died.

But if I was with someone else, someone who could be that block against other people intent on asking questions about how I am doing and if I've moved on with my life, then I might be able to stand the few hours required of me to fulfill my family obligation.

"Do you think it's too late for me to get one of

these temporary boyfriends for this weekend? I'm dreading the wedding more than I can say, Cheyenne."

Grabbing her enormous pink bag, she stuffs her hand in until her arm disappears up to her bicep. "I've got the number right here. It might be too late for this time, but maybe they can do something for you."

"How does this work?" I ask, imagining this process will be something like ordering off a menu at a restaurant.

Are they going to ask me what the man I want should look like? No, that's not possible. It's not like they're making clones of men for this. These are just escorts, so you have to take what they have.

At least that sounds right. Actually, I have no idea if that sounds right. I'm way out of my league on this, but if Cheyenne says it's good, then I trust her.

"So you have someone through this service for the wedding? What's his name?"

My sister smiles as she continues to rummage through that giant bag that's swallowed nearly all of her right arm. "Nico, although I'm pretty sure that's not his real name. I don't care, though. Hell, he can call himself whatever he wants as long as I don't have to get stuck dealing with the lecture from Mom about how I'm going to end up alone and with no one to take care of me when I get to be her age. I swear, if I have to listen to that tripe one more time, I'm going to explode and I won't be responsible for what I say to that woman, Savannah. Oh, here it is. I got it!"

She pulls out a torn envelope with some handwritten words scrawled on it and sets it on the table in front of me. Pointing at the phone number at the top, she says, "All you do is call this number and follow the prompts. It's easy. I swear. They'll ask you for details about what kind of event you need an escort for, and they even ask for what you'd like the man to look like. They can't be expected to always get you just what you want, if you get extremely specific, but they're always good looking and definitely presentable in front of family."

This sounds bizarre, but if it means I won't have to be at the wedding reception alone, it's worth taking the chance. I'd give anything to not have people staring at me like I'm some pathetic thing they'll be talking about for days after.

"How much is it?" I ask, not really caring how much this will cost. Some things are worth all the money you have.

"Five hundred, although since you're calling last minute, it might be more."

I take a deep breath in and close my eyes. I can do this. The alternative is a day full of sad stares from people and sitting along at the singles' table with my Aunt Grace listening to how she never met the man of her dreams but she's fine dying alone.

Staring down at the number, I pull my cell phone across the table to me. "Okay, let's do this! What's the worst that could happen?"

Cheyenne laughs at my question. "Nothing could be worse than another family event with everyone thinking you're sad. Make the call."

I press the numbers into my phone and listen for it

to ring. After only a second, a deep voice says, "Welcome. Please leave your name, your phone number, when you need our services, and any special event details. If you have any special requirements, please mention them also. We will get back to you soon."

A loud beep ends the man's speech, and I open my mouth to say something, but no words come out. It's like I'm suddenly unable to speak. So much for this being easy.

My sister nudges my arm and whispers, "Give them your info. Come on!"

My heart races, making my mouth dry, but I finally say, "My name is Anna Gardener, and I need an escort for this Saturday, September fifth. It's a wedding reception, black tie event, so the person will have to wear a tux."

I stop as I think about what I'd want this man to look like. All I can think of is Carson with his blond hair and green eyes.

No! I can't spend an afternoon with someone who looks just like him. I'll never be able to get through it.

So I blurt out, "I'd like the person to have dark hair and dark eyes."

Cheyenne whispers, "That was great!"

I feel like I need to explain myself, even though I don't know the person who will hear all this, so I add, "I just need someone with me so I'm not alone and have no one to deflect from my family. I guess that sounds sad, but if you come from a big family, you know what I mean. Thank you."

And with that pathetic explanation, I end the call and let out a heavy sigh. God, I hope the person who hears that doesn't think I'm too sad to hire someone. They don't have to spend the rest of their life with me. They just have to be my date for an afternoon.

"See? That wasn't so bad. But why did you say your name was Anna?"

"I don't know. I froze. He's going to know my name five seconds after we walk into the reception. God, that was stupid."

"It's okay. No big deal. You can say it's a nickname, if you want. Now when they call for payment, you have to use Bitcoin, so if you aren't sure how to do that, just ask me," Cheyenne says, trying to be supportive.

Except she makes me sound like I'm some old fool who doesn't know a thing about anything.

"You know, my husband was a wealthy man. It's not like I don't know about things like Bitcoin," I say more defensively than I meant to sound.

A smile lights up my sister's face, and she gets up to walk toward the kitchen. "Listen to you with the words. Gigolo and Bitcoin. Now we wait for your Mr. Right Now and our problems are solved, at least for this Saturday. In the meantime, I think it's time for a cocktail."

The way she says our problems will be solved by these temporary boyfriends makes me wonder if I should have tried to get back to dating before now. It has been two years since Carson died. He told me in no uncertain terms he didn't want me pining away for him after he was gone.

But am I even capable of loving another man after finding love with him?

CHAPTER FIVE

ash

SCRUBBING THE LAST OF THE NIGHT'S SLEEP FROM my face, I grab my phone and head out to the kitchen to make myself a cup of coffee and get my day started. Friday mornings are always busy, so I need to get my head together before my day rolls over me.

This weekend is Labor Day weekend, so the requests have been coming in fast and furious. I love making money, but I wish these women wouldn't wait until the last minute to decide they need our service. There are only so many of these guys to go around.

As I press the buttons on the coffee maker to get it going, I can't help but wish cloning was something available. That would solve all my problems. Clone a handful of my best guys a couple of times and voila! Everyone's happy.

I shake my head as the image of some freaky three-eyed dude pops into my brain. No, maybe cloning isn't a good idea.

Still, it would help with weekends like the one coming up.

After pouring a cup of coffee and throwing in a few spoonfuls of sugar, I head out to my balcony and take a seat to enjoy the last stage of waking up. Looking out over the city, I can't help but think it's nothing as good as Tampa. Gainesville isn't the worst place on earth, but it's not where my heart is.

It is where my money is, though, so for the meantime until at least next spring, this is where I get to stay. Not that I'm suffering here. I live in a great condo with all the bells and whistles and want for nothing. So, no, not exactly roughing it.

Ten minutes pass and with the final sip of coffee, I'm ready to face the day. I finished working last night with a request from a client for someone who looks like he plays professional football.

That one made me laugh. We don't get too many like that. I'm not sure what she meant, though. Linebacker size or tight end who can outrun even running backs. There's a pretty big difference there. Now if she said she wanted someone who looks like he plays in the NBA, that would have been easier. I'd send that job to Keyton, the only guy we have that reaches nearly seven feet tall. But football players are different.

Hopefully, she likes Rafe. He's pretty big, and although I'm not sure he's ever played football, the guy looks like he could lift a house with his bare hands.

I lift my phone to my ear and listen for the messages I left for today. There are only two. The first is a woman who wants an escort to an event in Miami Beach on Monday night. Thank you, Alyssa, for giving me some time on that one. Getting guys to drive hours south is one thing, but convincing them to do it last minute usually ends up in disappointment. Last resort, I have to take the job myself or cajole Damon into doing it, but since that means creating elaborate lies for his girlfriend so she won't find out, it actually means I end up with the assignment. That hasn't happened in a long time, thankfully.

Not that I wouldn't enjoy a night or two down there. I haven't been to Miami Beach in a couple months. Maybe if nobody bites at the job, I'll do it myself.

I jot down the first names who come to mind for it, though. Jace could work. He has a nice look to him that works well in big city settings. He sticks out like a sore thumb at backyard parties since he insists on wearing two thousand dollar suits everywhere he goes, but he would fit in nicely for this job.

Or Calvin. He's been asking for more work, and he does clean up nicely, especially when you find out he works on boats for his day job. Once he got the grease out from underneath his nails, he turned into one of our best guys.

The second message starts and I hear a soft voice say her name is Anna. She needs an escort for a wedding reception. Easy job. Cakewalk. Lots of smiling and dancing, and although the food is rarely top-notch, it's usually not terrible.

Marcus could do this job. I listen to her say she'd like someone with dark hair and dark eyes and know he's the man for it. Plus, he looks damn good in a tux, which isn't as easy as it sounds. Some guys just look like oversized penguins, especially those with bulging muscles. Never a good look.

I move my phone away from my ear when I think she's finished talking, but then I hear something and quickly listen as she says, "I just need someone with me so I'm not alone and have no one to deflect from my family. I guess that sounds sad, but if you come from a big family, you know what I mean. Thank you."

For a second, my chest contracts against my heart. I know exactly what she means. I love my family more than they can even know, but having all those eyes on you can be a lot to deal with. I don't know how big Anna's family is, but as someone who comes from a family the size of the March and Jackson clan, I know dealing with them can be a chore.

Especially when you're trying to hide parts of your life from them and they expect to know every tiny detail of your existence.

She finishes talking and the message ends, so I set my phone down and get to work on arranging escorts for the two clients. Fifteen minutes after I put the call out, Jace comes back with a definite yes to the event in Miami Beach. He can't wait to take a little vacation and get paid at the same time.

Anna's request I send to Marcus because he's the only one who's right for this job. I consider Seth for a few seconds, but he's too young and something about the way her voice trembled when she said those last few words into the phone tells me she's vulnerable. Definitely Marcus.

When I don't hear back from him in thirty minutes, I text him again. He's never one to slack on jobs, but maybe he's sleeping in late this morning. I don't know what he does when he isn't working for us, but maybe he got himself a full-time job?

Finally, an hour later, he gets back to me as I sit waiting on my balcony drinking my second cup of coffee for the day. Looking down at my phone, I read his message. He's sorry, but he has to go to his mother's third wedding that day. Damnit. I really don't want so send Seth out on this one. I'll just have to put this job out on a regular cattle call and see who comes back at me.

One by one, I get the same message. I can't do it because of the holiday weekend. By the time I finish my second cup of coffee, I know I've got no one for this job. Not even Seth, who can't do it because he's in the middle of a move.

That only leaves Damon or me. Fuck, I hate weddings.

After cursing out my partner and his girlfriend, I message this Anna person with the name I use whenever I have to go out on jobs. It's not completely a lie, but then again, who cares, right? This is a business deal, not some romance just starting.

Hi Anna,

I'm Cash Lucas and I'll be your date for the wedding Saturday. I just need to know the time and where to meet you. I look forward to hearing from you.

Cash

While I repeat my angry words for Damon and come up with a few choice ones I haven't used yet for that girlfriend of his, Anna quickly texts back with her address and when I should meet her there. It goes like clockwork, as these things usually do, but then she texts once more, this time with a demand.

I hope you understand, but I have to do it this way. You have to drive my car to the event.

Normally, I prefer to meet at a neutral site and then drive separately from there. It's the safest way to go and nobody feels like they're putting themselves in any danger. However, something about this woman says this is merely an idiosyncrasy she needs indulged and not the beginning of some plan to drug me and harvest my organs in some swamp nearby.

At least I hope not.

So I text back I'm fine with that and kick back to relax until the next client needs a man. It's good work, if you can get it, even when you have to actually be the escort sometimes.

CHAPTER SIX

Cash

My Lexus rolls over the tan and brown pavers set in a herringbone pattern that reminds me of the driveway at my parents' house. That's where the similarity ends, though. The March family has money, but one look at Anna's house says she's got that times ten.

Or a hundred. Whatever the multiplier is, she's loaded.

I stop the car and step out to look at the gorgeous home in front of me. Cream color, it reminds me of a house that belongs in Europe with its dark brown stone façade that runs halfway up the front of the house and wrought iron railings on the balconies on the second floor. To the left, a four-car garage with all its doors closed connects to the home, and in front of the door on the far right sits a silver Mercedes. By the looks of it, I suspect it's not even two years old and doesn't look like it's been anywhere but this courtyard.

Maybe this Anna woman is a shut-in who rarely goes out. The image of a woman like that one in Driving Miss Daisy pops into my head. That might not be too bad. I don't usually enjoy hanging out with elderly women, but it does tend to make the job easier, especially if she's cool like my grandmother.

I chuckle as the thought of Alexandria March hiring an escort to take her places runs through my head. She'd totally be all in for that. Grandma knows how to have a good time, and from what Alex and Cade told me a while back, she's definitely got some tricks up her sleeve, at least in her past.

So I get to be an old woman's stud for the afternoon. Again, it's not bad work, if she's as nice as she sounded on the phone, and at least there will be free booze and a meal at the reception.

When I walk up to the door, I see someone dart past the glass around it. Although it's just a quick glance, Anna doesn't seem to be an infirmed old lady. That's good. It might mean she wants to dance today, but that's not a bad thing. Some of these elderly women really know how to light up the dance floor, and assuming she's in good shape, I'm game.

I lift my hand to press on the doorbell, but the front door opens before I can and standing there isn't an old woman at all but a woman who looks to be about my age. Dressed in a dark blue strapless gown and wearing a diamond choker around her neck that highlights how she's put her dark hair up in a bun on the back of her head, she's stunning.

And definitely not what I expected.

Or maybe she's coming with us as a guest of Anna? I'm not sure at first, so I simply introduce myself and hope she explains who she is so I don't have to ask.

"I'm here for Anna," I say with a smile.

She looks confused for a moment, so I add, "I'm her escort to the wedding today."

"I know. I'm the one who hired you. I'm Anna Gardener."

Now I'm the one who's speechless.

When I don't say a word for nearly ten seconds, she covers her hand with her mouth and in a horrified voice says, "Oh my God! I'm so sorry. I wasn't supposed to say I'm paying you, was I? That makes it sound like you're a prostitute, but that's not what they call men who do this, is it? They call you gigolos, but I'm so sorry because that's not what this is."

Unsure I caught most of what she said, I just shake my head and smile. "No, it's okay. I wouldn't suggest mentioning any of that in front of your family, assuming you don't want them to know you hired me, but I'm fine with most of what you said. Except the gigolo part."

That makes her cover her entire face with her hands, and from behind them, she says quietly, "I am blowing this, and we aren't even out the front door. Maybe we could start again?"

I extend my hand and smile, hoping she can see

from behind her fingers. "Hi, my name is Cash Lucas. It's nice to meet you."

She slowly lowers her hands to reveal her cheeks are pink with a beautiful blush. Her dark eyes avoid meeting my gaze when she touches my hand and says, "Hi, I'm Anna Gardener. It's very nice to meet you too, Cash."

Her skin is petal soft against my fingers, and her handshake is as light as air. I look down at where our hands are joined and notice her skin is flawless. Then I feel her hand begin to tremble against mine.

"This is going to be okay. I promise. We're just two people going to a wedding reception, right?" I say, trying my best to calm her fears.

For the first time, she looks up at me and meets my gaze with her deep brown eyes. "I'm sorry I'm acting so stupid. I've just never done anything like this before."

"It's okay. Most people I work with haven't either. You look gorgeous, so you can feel great about that. I wear a tux pretty well, if I do say so myself, and everyone at this wedding is going to be wondering who I am and not focused on you. If you want me to say anything in particular to anyone in particular, just tell me. I'm here to make this easy for you."

"Thank you. You have no idea what my family is like. I hope they don't swamp you with questions. They've been pretty good at leaving me alone, but I couldn't get out of this wedding," she says, basically apologizing for something that hasn't happened yet.

I know what she means, though. Big families can be a lot to handle.

"Well, while we're on our way, I'll tell you about my family and you'll see it's not just yours that can be a bit much. Try five children born in five years to three brothers. Throw in an adoption and one more and that's just the kids in mine. Those three brothers each have a wife who's as different as night is to day, and there's the family matriarch who doesn't take no for an answer and doesn't seem to know she's supposed to slow down in her eighties. We're quite the bunch."

Anna's smile broadens as she listens to my quick rundown of the March and Jackson crew. Taking my arm, she walks with me to the car and laughs at my joke about my family tree having a lot of squirrels in it because we're nuts.

"Thank you for understanding my nervousness, Cash. I'm just not used to dealing with people much anymore."

As I close her door and walk around to the driver's side of the car, I wonder what happened to this woman to make her pretty much housebound, from the way she's described herself. I was right about the car. When I open the driver's side to get in, she remarks that it hasn't been driven in nearly two years. That detail, combined with her comment that she doesn't know how to deal with others anymore, makes me think something terrible happened to her.

Maybe an attack? Jesus, if that's the case, I need to make sure I don't make any sudden moves that she might interpret the wrong way. The last thing I need is to end up in handcuffs trying to explain today's arrangement between the two of us to one of Gainesville's finest.

When I slide in behind the wheel, I decide I need to be very careful with this woman. I can't risk my entire business on one person, so she gets the cool Cash this afternoon.

I put the car in drive and begin to roll down the driveway between the two enormous palm trees as she says in a quiet voice, "My husband died two years ago. That's why I seem so odd. I'm really not weird like this with people. I just haven't socialized much since he died. He was the only person to ever drive this car."

Gently, I slow the car to a stop and turn to look at her. She looks so vulnerable, so fragile staring at me, her eyes wide with something that looks like fear. I want to say maybe we should go in my car since I have a feeling this one brings with it a world of memories, but I don't.

Instead, I say, "I promise I'll take good care of it, Anna. It's in the best hands possible, I swear."

When I finish, she lets out a sigh like she's been carrying the entire world on her shoulders and for the first time in ages, it's been lifted from them. "Thank you for being so good about this and me and how weird I am. I know you probably do this just for the money, and I can appreciate that. I just want you to know you're being really sweet and I loved that story about your family."

"Well, I have hundreds more if you want to be bored. Just say the word, and I'll start talking."

She gives me a warm smile and nods. "I'd like that very much. Thank you, Cash."

And with that, Anna opens up Pandora's Box of March and Jackson family stories. I just hope she doesn't regret it.

I TAKE ANNA'S HAND IN MINE AND WE START walking to the Courtright Meadows Country Club main building. It's a beautiful, sunny September afternoon, and after our drive here and my stories about how my brother and my cousins and I terrorized our parents as little boys, she's finally calm enough so her hands aren't shaking.

This will be fine. It's just a wedding reception, and if I can handle my family, I certainly can handle hers.

And then from under the portico, a woman who looks like I imagine Anna would if she was twenty years older, fifty pounds heavier, and angry comes storming toward us like she has a bone to pick with either Anna or me. So much for thinking that everything would be smooth sailing.

"Where have you been? We've been waiting forever for you!" she announces loudly enough for anyone within twenty yards to hear. "Who is this? I thought you were coming alone. When did you start dating? Or is this just a friend?"

Anna squeezes my hand so tightly, I wonder if she's hurting herself. Knowing she's already probably spinning out of control, even after all that laughing she did in the car, I lean in toward her as we keep walking forward and say, "It's okay. Families are like this sometimes. Everyone has someone like this to deal with, and I'm here."

With each step, her grip on my right hand lessens so by the time the loud woman reaches us, Anna and I are simply holding hands and not holding on for dear life.

"Cash, this is Cecile, my older sister. Cecile, this is Cash Lucas, a friend of mine."

Her voice shakes on the final few words of her introduction, but I don't think her sister notices because her attention is fixed on my face. If that's what it takes for her to not pester Anna, so be it. I don't mind a little staring for a good cause.

"It's wonderful to meet you, Cecile. You look lovely in that green gown. It flatters you," I say with a smile, even as I think the truth is she looks like a large plant someone should prune.

"Did you know my sister's husband or did she meet you after?" Cecile asks.

Out of the corner of my eye, I see Anna wince like every word out of her sister's mouth is painful. I barely know this Cecile woman, but I already dislike her.

"I'm afraid I never had the good fortune to meet your late brother-in-law, but his reputation is well-known, so I know of his business success."

"And what do you do?" she asks, barely taking a moment to hear what I had to say to her first question.

Beside me, I can feel Anna's entire body tense up. We never discussed what my answer to that would be, so I have to go with what I usually tell people away from Tampa what I do for a living.

"I'm part owner of a restaurant."

More than just a tiny lie, but since my father and I share a name, I can usually get away with it. The fact that I use my mother's maiden name for my last name complicates things a bit in this situation, but if Cecile decides to do a little online stalking of me, it'll take her longer than one afternoon to figure out none of what I've told her is actually true.

By that time, Anna will be back home safe and sound and I'll be back to my life running my business with Damon.

When she asks what the name of the restaurant is, she's interrupted by another woman and a man walking toward us. I recognize the man instantly as Nico, one of my guys who works for us. He, of course, doesn't recognize me since Damon and I stay completely anonymous, but I can't help but smile that two women at this reception are paying my company.

"Cecile, they want you inside. Something about the ice sculpture melting and they need your personality to firm it back up," the woman says with a completely straight face.

Anna's older sister turns on her heel and snaps something at the woman before looking back and getting one last comment in. "I'm glad you're finally getting out. Just because your husband died doesn't mean your life has to end. He believed that, and I do too, so it's good to see you."

I feel Anna's hand reach for mine when her sister

finishes speaking, and I give it a gentle squeeze to let her know she's not alone. "Well, I hope we aren't sitting with her."

The woman with Nico smiles at me and then sweetly cradles Anna's face. "Now that the wicked witch is gone, I think we can go to the singles' table positioned somewhere between the bathroom and the kitchen, right?"

For the first time since we arrived, Anna smiles and her face lights up. Turning to face me, she says, "Cash, this is my younger sister Cheyenne."

"Good to meet you, Cheyenne."

As she shakes my hand, she rolls her eyes and says, "Sorry about Cecile. She's a royal bitch, but she's family so we have to deal with her. Everyone, this is Nico. He's probably horrified by that little show our sister put on, so why don't we go inside and find the bar? I definitely need a drink."

When the two of them walk away, Anna sighs and looks over at me. "You're probably thinking you should be getting paid twice your rate for this, I bet. I don't blame you. This is why I hate weddings."

"As long as we're sitting with your younger sister and not your older sister, I think we'll be fine. The singles' table is usually the best in the house."

Not exactly the way I thought this job would go, but so far, at least it hasn't been boring.

CHAPTER SEVEN

Savannah

BY THE TIME WE FINISH OUR DINNER, I KNOW I have to admit the truth about what my real name is to Cash. I didn't think things through when I lied on the phone initially, and since we've been sitting at a table for the past hour with a place card that has my real name written on it in bold black ink, I can't keep pretending I'm some woman named Anna.

When everyone around us heads out onto the dance floor, I take a deep breath and finally turn toward him to make my confession. "I guess you know my name isn't Anna."

Cash gives me a sly smile and glances over at the place card. "The choice was either that you got it wrong or they did."

"I didn't think it through when I said my name was

Anna. I've never done this before. I guess it's pretty obvious I'll never be a criminal mastermind."

"It's okay. You didn't exactly lie since Anna is technically part of your name. Savannah is a nice name too, though."

Hanging my head in humiliation, I mumble, "Thanks. It's a family name."

A family name from a family full of people I wish I didn't have to see at this moment. So far, my sister Cecile has come over twice to rudely give her opinion on my dress and how I'm wearing my hair, and my mother have ventured over to the table to simply stare at Cash and Nico, likely amazed her two youngest daughters aren't sitting alone trying to drink themselves into oblivion.

I should have found a way to avoid this day. Cash is nice enough, which is a blessing because if he wasn't, this would be a complete nightmare, but I feel ridiculous. Everyone here thinks I'm with him, and all I can think is I'm betraying my husband.

God, I'm pathetic.

It would be one thing if I was out of my mind and couldn't grasp the reality that Carson is gone. I'm not insane, though. In fact, I know all too well that my husband died two years ago and since then I've made myself practically a hermit. Crazy people at least have an excuse to be pathetic. They're crazy.

I'm just sad.

"Would you like to dance?" he asks, pulling me from my thoughts.

Torn with how guilty I feel for being here today

with anyone, not just Cash, and wishing I wouldn't feel this way, I take a deep breath and nod. "That might be nice. Thank you."

As we walk out to the dance floor, he says quietly, "I thought a slow song might be better."

Slow song. Fast song. It doesn't matter. Anything to take me out of my own head so I don't think about how wrong this all feels.

I don't recognize the song, but it seems many of the guests do, because the dance floor gets crowded. That's a good thing because if it was just the two of us out here, it would feel like we were on display.

It doesn't take long to see Cash knows how to dance. Smiling, I look up at him as he turns me away from my mother and Cecile standing on the edge of the dance floor.

"I'm afraid I'm not as good at this as you are, so if I step on your toes, please forgive me."

With a nod, he smiles back at me. "You wouldn't believe me if I told you how I learned how to dance. By the way, I think your mother and sister are trying to get their husbands out here, so be prepared."

Looking around, I see Cecile tugging on her husband Jacob's arm trying to pry him away from the bar on this side of the room. I know my brother-in-law, and he has no intention of dancing. He attends these things solely for the alcohol, and my sister knows that too. If she thinks she's going to change him now after ten years of marriage, she's out of her mind.

As for my father, while he might give in to my mother, he's busy playing the mayor of the reception, glad-handing everyone he sees come near his table. That's his style, though. My father loves to put his arms around you and pull you close while he tells some stupid joke or brags about his golf game. If he comes out to dance, I suspect it would be only to talk to other people and not to spend time with my mother, which he assiduously avoids at all times.

Turning back to face Cash, I shake my head. "I think we're safe. Jacob and my father have other goals for this reception than to spy on me. My brother-in-law and I haven't said more than a polite hello and goodbye in the decade he's been part of the family, so he doesn't care one whit what I'm doing, and my father is the type of dad who doesn't want to think of his daughters with anyone. It's like I'm perpetually stuck being eight years old in my father's eyes."

Before he gets the chance to change the subject away from how he learned how to dance, I add, "So tell me the story of who taught you to dance so well. Mother or sister? I'm guessing sister."

That makes him laugh. "Neither. I don't have any sisters, and my mother doesn't really dance. It was one of my aunts. Abbi, my Uncle Kane's wife. I was in eighth grade and there was a big dance at my school. I had the biggest crush on a girl named Kasey. Kasey and Cash. Looking back, I can see it was doomed just because of our names."

"That sounds adorable. Kasey and Cash. You must have been too cute together," I say as he slowly turns me toward the other side of the dance floor where

Cheyenne and her date seem to be getting quite cozy with one another.

"She was adorable. I wanted so much to be manly, but I didn't know how to dance and I knew there would be at least one slow dance that night. I didn't want to blow it, so I told my parents and they shipped me over to my aunt and uncle's house."

"So is your aunt a dancer?"

Cash's expression twists into one that looks like he doesn't want to tell me the truth, so I quickly say, "It's okay. If you don't want to tell me because that's not what happens with what you do, that's fine."

Shaking his head, his frown disappears. "Oh, no. It's not that. It's just…how can I phrase this correctly? She was a dancer, but not the type your family would appreciate."

I feel my cheeks heat up and know I'm blushing, even though he didn't say anything even close to risqué. Quickly, I try to show him I'm not as prudish as my face seems to indicate.

"That sounds so exciting. Please don't take my blushing as a sign you offended me. It must be so cool to know someone who was that free that she had the confidence to dance like that."

"My aunt is sweet, and to look at her, you'd never guess she did that. It was only for a short time, but she was the one who taught me to dance. Kasey and I ended up having that one slow dance, and then she never talked to me again."

A laugh threatens to escape from me as I listen to the end of his story and watch him practically pout as he recalls that night. I bury my head in his shoulder to hide how funny he looks now years later as he tells it, not wanting to offend him.

"I'm sorry. I'm sure you were heartbroken back then."

I lift my head and see him smiling down at me. "I was, but I've recovered. I'm just glad I got you to laugh with that story. If I knew that's what it took, I would have started telling you stories of my many teenage heartbreaks hours ago."

"Well, since you made me smile, why don't I tell you about my family so you can get a good laugh?" Tapping on the front of his shoulder, I say, "Behind you, left side, is my Aunt Linda. She's my father's sister, and she and my mother have this thing that when they get together, they seem like they're being nice, but if you listen carefully and watch what their eyes do, you know there's nothing good happening."

Cash glances over his left shoulder at my aunt with her hair up in a bun on the top of her head that looks like someone placed a big blond doughnut up there. Dressed in a red gown that's intended to highlight her breast implants, she reminds me of some country singer wannabe.

He looks back at me and opens his eyes wide. "No missing her, I guess. So what do they say to one another?"

I think back to the last time I got to witness the spectacle of my aunt and mother together. The time when she announced she was adding a boob job to her list of plastic surgery.

"Well, when she turned fifty, my aunt decided that she needed a tune up. That's what she called it. A tune up. What that meant was she was going to get a tummy tuck and some liposuction. When she mentioned it around all of us, my mother said, 'Well, that's lovely, Linda. It seems truly appropriate after years of trying to change your body with exercise.' You could hear a pin drop when the last word came out of her mouth."

Cash looks down at me, his own mouth hanging open at that part of the story like all of us looked that day at my mother's house. "What did your aunt say?"

Giggling, I explain, "No kidding, she didn't miss a beat. Turning to look at my mother, she said, 'Well, Karen, it's no crime to want to improve yourself. You should try it. I'm sure my brother would appreciate it greatly.' And again, there was nothing but complete and utter silence. You could cut the tension around us with a knife. And you know what? They never stopped smiling, the two of them, the whole time."

"I guess the knives come out when those two ladies are around," he says with a chuckle.

"So you see, I'm thinking my family is worse than yours."

The slow song winds down and some typical wedding reception song that involves a silly dance comes on, so we walk back to the table as he tries to convince me my family is about the same as his. "We don't have anything like your aunt and mother in my family, but I can tell you that I heard stories about two of my aunts not talking for a while back before all the kids came along. My father talks about that like it was some kind of Middle East peace summit that had to be brokered."

When we get to the table, no one else has returned, so it's just Cash and me. "Well, all I know is families can be a lot to handle," I say, happy this reception is almost over, even as I have to admit I'm having a good time with him.

"No doubt, but can you really imagine your life without them?"

Just then, my sister Cecile pops up out of nowhere and sits down next to me. Before I turn to face her, I whisper to Cash, "I can imagine my life without some of them, yes."

I scan the room for Cheyenne, desperate for her unique brand of sass at this moment since I have a feeling Cecile is about to pry into my business and I never have a snappy comeback for her when she does that. My younger sister is nowhere to be found, though, so I'm on my own, I guess.

"Are you having a good time, Cecile?" I ask, hoping to charm her into being nice. Or at least nicer than her usual self.

Completely ignoring my well-meaning question, she asks one of her own. "Don't you hate dancing? I saw you out there with your friend here, but I always thought you hated to dance. You used to say that whenever any of us asked why you and Carson weren't out on the dance floor like we wanted you to be."

I sheepishly look over at Cash, hoping he doesn't

think I hated to dance with him. Why does my sister have to be so nasty all the time? Couldn't she just dial it back for one afternoon?

"I don't hate dancing," I answer quietly, dreading the rest of the answer I know I have to give to stop her from talking about this subject. "Carson didn't like to dance because he didn't think he was very good at it, so I didn't press the issue."

She smiles like anything I said should please her, and for a moment, I can't help but think she looks like the Joker from the Batman movies with her red colored lips turned up into a vicious grin. God, where is Cheyenne?

"Well, there you go. I thought he was always perfect, but now the truth comes out. He was just a mortal man like the rest of us have."

My sister's jealousy regarding our husbands has never been a secret she's tried to keep under wraps. I know that, yet still to hear her talk about a dead man like she gets some kind of glee from knowing he had flaws makes responding to her impossible. The words get stuck in my throat, and nothing comes out.

From my right, Cash leans over and clears his throat before saying, "You know, I think a man who was wildly successful in the hotel business, along with having a beautiful wife and a gorgeous home can afford to have a few imperfections. I'm sure Savannah would put Carson up against any of the men in this room and still come out on top."

For a few seconds, my sister doesn't say a word and I'm not even sure I heard Cash correctly. She huffs out her disgust at his comment and storms away in her usual style, sure to return with more cruelty another time.

But for now, I can't express how much I appreciate what Cash said to her.

"Thank you. You have no idea how much I wish I could say things like that when she's so mean. I know I should just ignore her when she's being petty, but I can't. The problem is I can't respond the way you did either."

"Sounds like a case of jealousy to me. I'm sure she's going to be hating me now too, but that's okay. I'm glad I could help there."

I want to say so much more, but instead I just look into his blue eyes and hope he understands how much what he said meant to me. He really is a gorgeous man, inside and out.

Cheyenne returns to the table with Nico and drops a bag of candy in front of me. "Cecile just left, so of course, you need something sweet to wipe away the taste of her words," she says with a smile.

"Thanks, but I think I need to find the ladies' room. Why don't you come for a walk with me and Cash and Nico can talk about man stuff?" I say as I stand from the table.

Cheyenne and I have had that code since we were girls, so she knows I don't really need to visit the ladies' room. What I need to do is talk to her, and she picks up on my hint instantly.

"Time for us to go powder our noses, gentlemen.

Be right back!" she announces before giving Nico's bicep a squeeze.

We have to wait for two older women to finish before we have the bathroom to ourselves, and when they finally leave, I turn to Cheyenne practically beaming. "This was such a good idea. Thank you for suggesting I call that number. Cash has been really great today."

My sister bites her lip and smiles. "Nico is the best money I've spent in a long time. I can't stop touching him. He's so fine. I got very lucky when they sent me him. I think half the women in this place are jealous of me, and the other half are jealous of you because of Cash."

"Cecile came over a few minutes ago and started in on how Carson wasn't perfect after all because he couldn't dance well. She's so awful."

Cheyenne rolls her eyes while she checks her makeup in the mirror. "The word you're looking for is bitch, Savannah. I swear, I don't know how we're related to her, you know that? Did Mom have an affair with the mailman to get us?"

I watch her fix her mascara, eager to tell her that this time our older sister didn't just get to have her say and stroll away like always. "But Cash snapped right back at her. You should have heard him. He said that Carson had such a great life that he could afford to have a few flaws. Well, it wasn't exactly that. I'm paraphrasing. But that was the sentiment, and Cecile had nothing to say back to him. He shut her up completely. It was so great!"

Finished with her face and hair, she turns to look at me and pushes a stray hair that's escaped from my bun. "That's terrific. It's about time we all started doing that to her. She's such a bitch."

"He really was fantastic. I was looking for you the minute I realized she was coming my way, but he handled her. Even Carson never handled Cecile like that."

Cheyenne tilts her head and stares at me for a long moment. "That's because Carson thought she was beneath him and you. He'd never deign to bother with her. Savannah, I want you to be careful not to get attached to Cash. I know he handled Cecile, which you know I approve of wholeheartedly, but he's paid to be here. He's not a real boyfriend, honey."

Embarrassed my younger sister feels like she has to remind me of that fact, I lower my head to avoid her intense gaze. "I know. I just really liked how he handled her."

"Well, that's good. Then he's an escort who's earned his money. Nothing more. Now let's get back to the table before one of those bridesmaids of Daria's steals my guy away. He's mine to touch for tonight."

I watch Cheyenne flash her reflection a smile before walking out of the ladies' room and know she's right. I can't let myself get attached to Cash. It's just that I've been alone for so long that it's nice to be around someone who likes me and stands up for me with Cecile.

Then again, he's paid to act like he likes me. He is an escort, after all.

CHAPTER EIGHT

ash

AFTER A LONG DAY OF WEARING A TUX AND pretending not to hate weddings as much as I truly do, I set my feet up on the ottoman and close my eyes, happy to be back in a pair of shorts and a t-shirt to relax. The next time I think I should go out on a job instead of making sure someone else takes it, I need to remember how my feet felt in those shoes for all those hours.

I stretch my arms above my head and try to work the day out of my muscles. If you don't think too much about them, weddings seem like a nice thing, but when you're working one dressed in a tux and forced to be around people you don't know from a can of paint, they're much harder than they appear on the surface.

This beer Damon brought over last week feels good going down, but it's going to take a lot more of these babies to lull me into the state I'd love to reach right now. First thing tomorrow morning, I need to go through the applications we have so I don't have to be anyone but the guy who's half owner of the business and the one who schedules assignments.

When I finish that bottle, I walk back into the kitchen and grab a second, wishing anything but gin or vodka could do the job but knowing whatever import beer Damon's fallen in love with recently isn't up to the challenge tonight. I'm not in the mood to drive to the store to restock my bar, though, so beer will have to do.

I turn on a baseball game and let my mind wander as the Marlins run all over the Mets. I'm not really interested in really watching the game, too busy thinking about Savannah and that family of hers.

As much as I wanted to convince her they're like mine, Jesus Christ are they worse. That sister Cecile needs to be put in her place, but as much as I enjoyed giving her a little bit of her own medicine, I wasn't the one for the job. Her sister Cheyenne is far more likeable. Nico and she looked like they were having a good time. I wonder if she decided to offer him something above and beyond his expected duties today.

Closing my eyes, I see the image of Savannah smiling up at me as we danced, one of the better parts of the day. She's sweet, especially compared to everyone around her. She's also more vulnerable than I usually like in a woman. Broken is not my thing.

As the thought of her lingers, my phone rings, interrupting my replay of my time with her. I look over on the table and see Alex's name on the screen. What time is it? Isn't he usually working on Saturday nights? Isn't that a big time for the restaurant?

Grabbing it, I answer the call, joking, "Hey, did Dad and Kane finally let you have a single Saturday night off? I'd think you'd have better things to do than call your big brother to chat, though."

Unlike usual when I bust his ass, Alex doesn't laugh. In fact, he doesn't say anything for a few seconds, and I wonder if the call's still live.

"You there? Prank calls don't really work anymore, especially when your name comes up on the other person's cell phone, man."

"Sorry, I was listening to Dad say something. Cash, Mom's been rushed to the hospital. Dad found her unconscious when he got home from the restaurant tonight. He wanted me to call you to let you know. We're here at Tampa General now."

His words hit me like a sledgehammer to the chest. My mother unconscious? All I can think of is her lying somewhere in their house, the house I grew up in that is so much her.

Choking down my emotions, I head toward the bedroom to get dressed to leave. "When did this happen, Alex?"

"They don't know how long she was out for. I've been here for about fifteen minutes trying to find out something more before I called you, but they don't seem to know anything yet. They're running tests. Cash, Dad's a mess. He's pacing back and forth up and down the hallway one minute and then sitting in the nearest chair staring off into space the next. He's worried. I am too. I think you should drive down tonight."

I've slipped on a pair of jeans and tossed enough clothes for a couple days in a bag by the time he finishes talking. Throwing it over my shoulder, I hurry out into the living room to find my wallet and keys.

"I'm on my way. I just need to make a call, but I can do that while I'm driving."

"Okay. Good. I think we need you here. I have to call Kane and Stefan. No, I already called Kane. I mean Cade. Fuck, I'm a mess too, I guess. Well, let me go and I'll see you in a couple hours, right?"

My brother sounds like he's falling apart. I've never heard Alex like this. Is there something he isn't telling me?

"Yeah, I'll be there as fast as I can. I've made it back home in ninety minutes before, so I can do it again. Hey, Alex, is there something else I should know?"

I can't bring myself to say it, but all I can think about is my mother on the floor, alone while some horrible disease takes over her body. Why was she unconscious? Did something happen to make her not have enough oxygen?

Fuck, if that's what happened, she might never wake up.

Shaking my head, I push that terrible thought away. I can't think like that. No. She's going to be okay. She's always been okay. Now's no different.

"I don't know anything more, Cash. Just get here, okay? I'll see you in a little while."

"I'm leaving now. I'll see you soon, Alex. Tell Dad I'm coming, and if you need me to stop to get anything for Mom or him or you, whatever you need, just call."

By the time I end the call, I'm leaving my apartment. The Lexus can get me back to Tampa in ninety minutes, like I told him, but maybe I should see if I can get there even faster.

Hurrying out to my car, I call Damon to let him know I won't be around for a few days. He answers his phone like he's been waiting to hear from me.

"Hey, Cash! I thought I'd get a call from you tonight. How was it being back in the trenches today? I hope it wasn't too bad because that would suck."

At first I don't understand what the hell he's talking about. Sometimes Damon talks shit, but I don't get the reference. "What trenches?"

"The wedding reception," he answers with a chuckle. "Back in the tux and those shoes you used to bitch about. I bet it sucked, didn't it?"

I toss my bag into the back seat and slide in behind the wheel to start the car. "No, it wasn't too bad, I guess. I still hate the shoes, so yeah, that wasn't good. But that's not why I'm calling. I need to head back to my family for a few days, so I wanted to give you a head's up since I won't be around at least until Tuesday, I'm thinking. Maybe later. I don't know."

"Everything okay? You sound like shit. Nothing bad happened, did it?" he asks in that serious voice I rarely hear come out of his mouth. Even when it comes to business with us, he's always the joker compared to me.

As I head out of the parking lot behind my condo, I explain, "My mom's in the hospital. My father found her unconscious on the floor when he got home from work tonight. I'm driving back to Tampa right now."

"Aw, damn, Cash. I hope she's going to be okay. Your mom is a nice lady. Way nicer than my mother. I'll keep everything status quo here. You take care of your family. Let me know what happens, okay?"

"Yeah. I'll let you know as soon as I find out what the hell is going on. Right now, you know as much as I know, so I'm more than a little freaked out, to be honest. I was going to look through the new applications because after that wedding today, I can't avoid the fact that we need more guys to work, but that will have to stay on hold until I get back."

"Don't think about work. I've got that covered. You just focus on your family and the business will be here when you get back."

My business partner can be a real asshole sometimes, and that girlfriend of his makes working with him a challenge more often than I like, but when it comes right down to it, Damon's a good guy and a good friend. I need that right now in at least one part of my life.

"Thanks, man. I'll let you know what's going on as soon as I can."

"Got it. Take care, Cash."

Setting my phone on the console, I start the drive I've made more times than I can remember in the past two years. It's a straight shot down I-75, and if I can avoid the cops, I might be able to make it in record time tonight.

Damnit, she's got to be okay. She just has to.

I wrack my brain for anything she said to me the last few times we talked that could clue me in to what could be wrong, but nothing stands out. She didn't mention anything about having headaches any more than usual. Last weekend at Grandma's, I overheard her say to Dad that he was making her head throb, but that's nothing new. She says that all the time.

Did she look sick then? I don't think so. She looked the same as she always has. Pale skin with red hair and freckles. That's my mom. My grandmother says she has peaches and cream skin, which I used to think as a child referred to all that yogurt she ate every morning for breakfast. But she looks the same as she always has. Her dark eyes didn't look like they were cloudy or anything last weekend, but fuck, I wasn't exactly paying that close attention.

In fact, I spent the time back home trying to avoid her as much as possible because whenever she's around me, she wants to talk about that goddamned graduation party. Every time I turned around, there she was making plans for it. Who did I want to invite in addition to her and my father's friends? What food did I want served? How big a cake should she have made? All of it made me want to run away to avoid the reality I know I have to face up to soon.

Now I wish I just told her and Dad the truth.

The problem is they have their hearts set on me becoming a lawyer. It's all they've been able to talk about, other than me graduating from law school and passing the bar next year. I don't want to disappoint them, but will they ever understand how much I hated the life that lay ahead of me if I went through with law school?

I speed past cars in the right lane, red and white lights becoming a blur as I race back to my hometown and hope it's not too late for me to fix things. At this rate, I should make it there by a little before ten o'clock.

Ten o'clock. She used to insist Alex and I had to be in bed by that time when we were kids. I was eleven years old, and all I wanted to do was hang out with my father when he came home from work, but he didn't get back until right after ten every night. I'd pester her each day after dinner to let me, begging to be allowed to stay up since I was almost a teenager and Liam, who was thirteen by then, was always allowed to stay up later than ten at night.

"Mom, I need to talk to Dad about something, so can I wait up for him?" I ask as she takes my empty plate from the table.

Across from me, Alex looks up at her with hopeful eyes, wanting the same thing I do, but he's even younger than I am. She would never have let me stay up last year.

"Cash, you know how I feel about that. Boys your age need

their sleep. You won't be able to be your best in school tomorrow if you're up too late tonight," she answers, frowning at the repeat of our conversation from last night and the night before and every night for the past few months.

"I won't be tired tomorrow. I promise," I say, practically begging her to break her rule just for tonight.

The tryouts for baseball are coming up in a couple weeks, and I want my father to help me practice so I make the team again this year. He loves doing it, but he needs to know in advance so Uncle Kane can take over at the restaurant for the time he needs to be away.

My mother levels her gaze full of disbelief on me and scowls. "You don't know that. Staying up with throw your whole schedule off. Can't you just talk to your father the day after? He doesn't have to be at work until late Saturday afternoon, so you two can have a long talk about whatever you need to that morning."

I sit back in my chair, folding my arms across my chest in frustration. That's what she always says. Wait. Do it some other time. Why can't I ever get to do what I want when I want to do it?

While I stew in my anger, my brother picks up where I left off. "Please, Mom? You know we won't be tired if we stay up just a little late. Just a half hour. Honest. Please?"

Alex always likes to jump on my bandwagon the moment he senses I'm getting something he might like. I don't mind, and to be honest, my mother likes to spoil him, so she might say yes if he joins in with me. Whatever it takes. He's never been able to keep his eyes open past nine-thirty anyway, so even if he does get to stay up, I'll still be able to talk to Dad alone anyway.

My mother turns to look at him and smiles. "Oh, so now it's both of you wanting to stay up late? And what do you need to be up to ten o'clock for, Alexander March?"

Uh-oh. She's using his full name. Well, not his middle name. That's reserved for when he's in big trouble. When I hear her yell Alexander Cade March, I know it's time to close my door because he's about to get it. She doesn't say it often, but when she does, he's done something really bad.

"I want to stay up because Cash is staying up. I'm ten years old now, Mom. Ten year olds and eleven year olds should get to stay up later," he says like he's given this a lot of thought.

For a moment, she seems to think about our requests, likely because it's both of us. That's another reason why I don't mind when Alex joins in on something I want to do. Two against one are always better odds, and knowing she rarely says no to him helps my case.

Then she gets that face that tells me all hope is lost. It's a combination of her lips pursed and her eyebrows drawn in. She doesn't look angry as much as irritated.

"Maybe another night, boys. Right now, I need you to make sure your homework is done because you both need to get baths in. That show you like is on at eight, so you can watch that, but I want you both in bed by nine."

The way she runs through the laundry list of things she wants and totally ignores what I want makes something inside me snap. I don't care about my homework or taking a bath or watching whatever show she thinks I care about right now. All I want is to hang out with my father tonight when he gets home. Why won't she let me have that one tiny thing just this once?

Alex groans his disappointment before he slides his chair back and begins walking toward the stairs to start fulfilling all the tasks she wants done, but I don't move from the table. He looks over at me in confusion, like he can't understand why I'm not moving after hearing her say what she wants done.

Not tonight, Alex. Tonight, I'm going to get what I want.

"I already did my homework," I say defiantly, my arms still crossing my chest in the clearest sign of body language I can give her.

She stops rinsing off the dishes and looks over toward the table at me with a smile. "Good. Then you can get your bath in first since I think your brother still has some math work to do."

"I don't want to take a bath. I don't need a bath. I'm not dirty. I haven't done anything today that would make me need a bath."

The smile on my mother's face fades away, leaving her looking as confused as Alex did before he walked upstairs. "You need a bath, Cash. Every night. You know how this goes. We do this every night, so go up and get yourself in the tub. Or if you want, you can take a shower. Your father says that boys your age like showers, so feel free to do that tonight."

"I don't want a bath and I don't want a shower. I want to see Dad when he gets home tonight."

Now I sound more petulant than defiant, but I don't care how my words are coming out at this point. I'm tired of being treated like a baby. I'm eleven and I should be able to stay up until my father comes home from work so I can talk to him about practicing before baseball tryouts.

She doesn't respond immediately, instead taking her time to turn off the water and dry her hands on the dishcloth hanging next to the sink. The silence between us should frighten me, but it doesn't. Not tonight. Tonight, I'm going to get what I want and she's going to see I'm old enough to stay up late.

Walking out to the table, she takes a deep breath in and lets it out slowly. I've seen her do that many times before she says something that's on her mind. It usually is followed by the words, "Let me tell you this," and then she says the thing that's made her angry.

So I brace for whatever she has to tell me, still sure I'm not giving in. Tonight, she'll finally have to see I'm old enough to stay up.

"Cassian March, I'm not arguing with you about this. You aren't old enough to stay up that late on a school night. We've been through this time and time again, and the answer is the same as always. No. Your brother seems to understand what that word means. Why don't you?"

Her cheeks get all red as she talks, a clear sign she's angry. Good. I'm angry too, so maybe she'll understand me now.

"Alex is ten. I couldn't stay up late when I was ten, but I'm eleven now. Why can't I stay up to see Dad when he comes home? I'm not a baby anymore, Mom. Dad would let me if he was here. You know he would. So why can't I?"

"Because he's not here and I am, and I say no. That's why," she snaps, her eyes flashing how little patience she has for this conversation now.

But I'm going to give up as easily as I have all those other times.

"Well, I wish Dad was here so you could see you're not being fair. He'd tell you. He'd say it's okay for me to stay up, and then it would be both of us against you and you'd have to give in to what we want instead of me having to give in all the time."

When she doesn't immediately say anything, I think I've succeeded in changing her mind. Finally, I've figured out what to say that will work with her.

I silently congratulate myself for winning this battle, but a second later, I see hurt fill her eyes. That's how anyone can tell when my mother is upset about something. She gets this look in her dark eyes that says she's trying not to cry but she really wants to. Alex gets the same kind of look in his eyes when he's upset too. I've always assumed it must be because they both have brown eyes since my father and I never get a look like that in our blue eyes.

"I'm sorry you wish your father was here instead of me. That's just not possible, though, so you're stuck with me, fair or not. I need to get this place straightened up since you and your brother made a mess and didn't put everything away, so please go upstairs and take a bath."

Her tone is flat, like she's trying hard not to show any emotion. But it's in every word, and each one makes me feel guilty for what I said.

I don't know why, but that twists into something I know I shouldn't feel, and I yell at her, "I wish you would always be away and Dad could be the one who's here with us. Then Alex and I would finally be happy!"

I don't need to look into her eyes to know those words hurt her. The frown that looks like it will never go away tells me that. She doesn't say another word to me, and I run out of the room full of hate I don't understand for myself, her, what I *said, what she won't do, and too many other things that shouldn't matter at all but do.*

She doesn't come upstairs to check on us for another two hours. I spend the time hiding in my room, and when I hear her tell Alex good night and she loves him, I lock my bedroom door. I don't know why. Maybe I'm scared she'll yell at me since she's had time to think about all the terrible things I said. I don't know, but when she jiggles the handle and finds it locked, she doesn't say anything and simply walks away.

Fueled by spite and a feeling of guilt that grows by the minute, I force myself to stay awake until my father gets home. I perch myself at the top of the stairs hoping for a chance to talk to him like I wanted to, and I hear her tell him all the things I said to her. I listen as she sobs and he tries to reassure her that boys can be difficult at my age.

Tears fill my eyes and my breath gets caught in my chest when she says, "I just don't know why he hates me, Cassian. Alex never says things like that, but with Cash, it's like he's so full of anger when it comes to me that I don't know what to do."

My father again reassures her everything will be fine, and in the darkness, I whisper, "I don't hate you, Mom."

A car horn drags me back from the past, and I quickly check the car as it drifts over toward the right lane. I hate thinking back to those days when I was a young kid who didn't know how to control my emotions. My mother always got the worst of it too, even though I didn't mean most of what I ever said to her. She never mentioned a word about it to me after I made her cry all those times either.

Now she's lying in a hospital bed unconscious and

may never wake up. What if don't get the chance to tell her how sorry I am for being that terrible kid who made her cry? What if I don't get the chance to tell her the truth about what I've been doing for the past two years?

CHAPTER NINE

Cash

ALEX AND MY FATHER STAND IN THE WAITING AREA
on the third floor as I walk down the hallway toward
them. That's not a good sign. If she was resting
comfortably, at the very least my father would be in
the hospital room with her.

"I got here as fast as I could. What's going on?"

My father doesn't say a word and simply hugs me
to him. I wish he'd say something so I'd know what's
going on. Nothing has happened, has it?

"Hey, Dad. Tell me how she is," I say, my words
struggling to get out because I'm afraid of what the
news will be.

He sighs against me before dropping his arms
away from my back. Christ, I hate the look in his eyes.
I was wrong. It isn't something only Mom and Alex

82

get in their eyes. I see that look of sadness and hurt in his eyes now too.

"We're waiting for the doctors to tell us something. I don't know what happened. I came home from the restaurant and found her on the floor in the living room. I don't know how long she was there or what happened to make her fall. I tried to wake her up, but when that didn't work, I called the ambulance."

"It's going to be okay, Dad. Mom's strong. Whatever this is, she's going to be okay," I say, hoping I sound as positive as I want to.

I look over at Alex and see he's a mess too. "You look like you could use about ten hours of sleep. You okay?"

My brother shakes his head, and I can see he's barely keeping it together. "I just talked to her this afternoon, and she sounded fine. What could have happened?"

"Maybe low blood sugar? I was thinking that as I drove into the parking garage a few minutes ago," I suggest. "Doesn't Grandma have that? Maybe it runs in Mom's family."

I realize how unlikely that sounds, but Alex looks like he needs something to hang on to, some shred of hope he hasn't thought of yet. It seems to do the job, and he nods as if he likes that idea.

"Maybe. I hadn't considered that. I just know she was fine when I spoke to her this afternoon around two. She called the restaurant looking for Dad to tell him about the landscapers coming today, and she and I were joking about how he always says he wants to rip up all the grass and put down concrete everywhere. She laughed and swore…"

Alex doesn't finish his sentence, but he doesn't have to. All three of us standing there know what she said after that. "Over my dead body will he tear up all that beautiful green grass."

It's what she always says after joking about my father and his dream of paving over every square inch of the yard.

My father winces as those unspoken words fill his head. Turning away, he says quietly, "I swear to God if it was something with that grass, I'm going to finally have a reason to rip the whole fucking lot of it up."

My brother and I look at each other and shake our heads. Neither one of us seem to believe something happened to my mother because of the grass. I want to think it's something simple like that low blood sugar idea, but I have no idea.

That's the worst part of this. Driving here, all I could think about were all the things I want to make up for from the past and the million reasons that might explain what happened. It's torture not knowing.

Alex points toward the hallway where an older man dressed like a doctor walks toward us. "Dad, is this her doctor?"

My father spins around and stares in desperation at the man. "Do you know what's happened to my wife?" he asks in the saddest voice I've ever heard come from him.

Short and a little round, the doctor looks at the three of us and smiles. Pushing his wire-framed glasses up the bridge of his nose, he nods. "We found out what's going on, and I think she's going to be fine. It will take a couple days stay here, but with the right medicine, she'll be as good as new by week's end. Are there any cardiovascular issues in your family, Mr. March?"

My father looks relieved for a moment but when he shakes his head, the fear returns to his eyes. "Not that I know of. Her mother has issues with her sugar levels, and maybe her father had heart problems. I don't remember at the moment, to be honest."

"Well, it can be hereditary, but it doesn't always have to be. Your wife's heart misfired. Well, that's what I like to say. It stopped working for a few seconds, just long enough to make her fall unconscious. I know you said you didn't know how long she was out, but I'm thinking only a few minutes. She's awake now and has been for a while, but I wanted to run the tests to see if it could be anything else. As far as we can tell, it's just her heart."

Alex and I share glances as I try to figure out if this is good news or bad. The heart sounds bad, but my mother being awake is definitely good news.

"So what now? Can we see her?"

The doctor nods again. "Yes. It's after visiting hours, but I think if you three are very calm and very quiet, we can let you see her for a few minutes. I want her to get some rest tonight, though, so only a few minutes."

· · ·

85

WE FOLLOW HIM DOWN THE HALLWAY TO MY mother's room, and it's like I'm a little boy again. My body can't stop shaking from my fear of what she's going to look like lying there in that hospital bed and I can't seem to control my emotions.

I look over at Alex and see he's going through the same thing. The look in his eyes is that one he gets whenever he's upset. The one my mother got that night I was so cruel to her when I was eleven.

My heart races, slamming into my chest as I watch the doctor slowly push open the door to her room. I want to see her to let her know she's not alone and she has us here for her, but at the same time, a sense of dread fills me.

"Now just a few minutes, okay? Mr. March, the nurses have a chair set up for you if you want to say tonight, but just you. I want Olivia to stay as calm as possible."

Alex smiles at me, and in an attempt at something to lighten the mood, jokes, "Then our father is the perfect guy for the job. He does calm, cool, and collected like no one else on earth."

I give him a tiny smirk, worried if I let out any kind of laugh, it's going to sound wrong to everyone's ears. I follow my father and brother into the room, and the first sight I get of my mother makes my breath catch in my chest.

She looks so small in that bed. It's just a twin bed, so why does she look like she weighs ninety pounds tops. Her red hair against the white pillow behind her head looks like it always does, like a sign of that temper she hides behind her beautiful face, but her skin seems so pale now.

Stopping at the foot of her bed, I stand next to Alex and can practically hear his heartbeat along with mine. Our father moves over to the side of the bed and leans down to press a kiss to her forehead, but her eyes remain closed.

"Hey, baby. I'm here with the boys. You gave us quite a scare there," he says quietly, his voice shaking on the words baby and boys.

Slowly, she opens her eyes, and before she says a word, she makes a tiny smile. One by one, she focuses on each of us and then says in a voice barely above a whisper, "You all look so worried. It's okay. I'm better now."

My father pulls the chair up next to the bed and sits down to take her hand in his. Jesus, that looks pale and tiny too.

"You don't have to talk. I'm here and Cash and Alex are staying for a few minutes before they have to leave. But I'll be here all night with you, Liv."

She nods and then looks up at my brother and me. "Don't be worried, boys. The doctor says I'm going to be okay. I see in your eyes you're frightened, but you don't have to be. I'm going to be okay now."

I smile as she tries to reassure us, but I hate how she keeps saying okay. I don't want her to be just okay. I want her to be like she's always been. But what if okay is all she gets from now on?

"Alex, honey, you've got those eyes you get when you're upset. I promise, I'm fine. Honest. And Cash, stop frowning and doing that thing with your eyebrows you always do when you're unhappy. Everything's going to be okay."

So typical of her to be the one to make us feel better when we come to see her in the hospital.

"So did the doctor say you're going to have to follow some strict diet or anything?" Alex asks in a low voice. "Because when they spring you from this joint, I'm going to come over and make you a dinner you're going to never be able to forget. Hailey told me that she wants to make you a special dessert for your welcome home too. Cade told me she's already got the whole thing planned out."

My mother's smile lights up her face, and finally, she looks like herself again. Pushing herself up against the pile of pillows stacked up behind her, she sits up straight and shakes her head.

"Not that they told me, other than taking care of my cholesterol, but that's something anyone my age has to watch. Make it a surprise, honey, because I always love anything you make, especially when I don't know what to expect. And please tell Cade and Hailey I can't wait to see the dessert she makes. They're always so delicious that even if the doctors told me I couldn't have any sweet, I'd still sneak a bite."

"Don't worry," my father says, now looking genuinely relieved for the first time since we walked into the room. "I'm always up for indulging in whatever treats Hailey sends over, so if your mother doesn't eat them, I will."

I smile, relieved my mother appears so much more like herself with every second that passes, and she looks up at me like she's worried I might feel left out. "Don't worry, Cash. This little bump in the road isn't going to affect any of the plans for your graduation party. I have a few months to get everything set up, so it's going to be wonderful, just like I promised."

"Don't worry about that now, Mom. That kind of stuff can wait. The most important thing is the doctors figure out how to make sure this doesn't happen again. You're what we worry about, not some party."

Behind us, the hospital door opens and a nurse quietly announces, "I'm sorry, but Mrs. March needs her rest. Visiting hours start at eleven tomorrow morning, so you can come back then."

As much as we all want to stay, Alex and I nod our understanding. "Well, they're throwing the kids out. Parents only tonight, Mom," my brother says.

"Come give me a kiss goodnight. It'll be like when you were little boys and I'd tuck you into bed, except now I'm the one in bed."

Alex walks around the left side of her bed and leans over to kiss her. "I'll be back tomorrow, Mom. Try to get some sleep."

She cradles his face in her hands and smiles up at him in that way she always has with my brother. "I love you, sweetheart. Don't worry about me, okay?"

When I reach her, she has a very different expression on her face, like she's worried about me instead of the opposite. "Cash, I hate that you had to drive all the way down here for nothing. I hope this didn't take you away from studying for an exam."

God, I hate looking down into her dark eyes so full of concern for me while she's the one lying in the hospital bed, especially since everything she's worried about doesn't even exist. My life is one big lie, and here my mother is after falling unconscious because of her heart afraid she's interrupted something more important than being here to see her.

"Mom, it's okay. Exams come and go. You're my mother. I couldn't let you be in the hospital and not come here to see you."

That gets me a huge smile. "You're such a good kid, Cash. You always have been."

I try to smile, but the memory of how awful I was to her that night and the other times I thought I should push my limits with her reverberate in my mind. "Get some rest, and I'll be back with Alex in the morning. I expect to see you back to yourself, all right?"

"You sound like you should be a doctor, not a lawyer," she says with a tiny giggle. "I love you, honey. Go get some sleep so you don't spend the whole night doing that frowning thing you do. I'll see you two tomorrow."

I lean down and kiss her on the forehead. "Love you, Mom."

"I'm staying here tonight but I'm not going to want to spend much of it on the phone, so if you two can send out the alert to the rest of the family, that would be great," my father says as we move toward the door. "Don't forget your grandmother. If she doesn't know all about how your mother is doing by the time she wakes up in the morning, I'll never hear the end of it."

"I'll call her on my way home, Dad," Alex says. "Cade too, and he'll make sure Stefan and Shay know what's going on."

"And I'll call Kane and Abbi, so that branch of the family will be in the loop," I say.

Suddenly, my mother's expression twists into one of pure worry. "Oh, Cash, honey. Where are you going to stay? I didn't change the sheets in your bedroom this week. I didn't get a chance before this happened."

So typical of my mother to think that's the most important thing to consider right now.

"Well, I can sleep on the sheets you put on after the last time I stayed in my old room, Mom. Unless you've been renting the place out to strangers, I'm the only person who sleeps in that bed."

Alex slaps me on the back to get my attention. "He's staying at my place tonight, so don't worry about the sheets," he says with a smile.

Surprised to hear him offer, I nod my head so my mother thinks it's all been decided. "See? No problem with the sheets at all. We'll be back tomorrow morning. Have a good night, you two."

I don't know why, but my mother blushes at that. "Yeah, we're going to be having a grand old time with me in this bed and your father sleeping in a chair."

My brother and I turn to look at each other and shake our heads. Rolling his eyes, Alex says, "Did she just make a joke implying we thought they were going to be having sex here tonight?"

That makes her burst out laughing, and she covers her face with her hands. "Alex! I swear I don't know where you come up with the things you say. You two better go before I die of embarrassment."

My father's face registers his reaction to that word die, but he forces a smile and waves us away. "Go before the doctor comes in and wonders why we're all still in here. We'll see you tomorrow morning. Have a good night."

As Alex and I walk down the hallway toward the door out to the parking garage, I have to laugh. "At first, I was a little freaked out there. She looked bad. Leave it to Mom, though, to be thinking you're making sex jokes by the time we're going."

"She did look bad," he says with a frown. "But she got better while we were there, so that's good. I meant what I said about you staying with me, Cash. It'll be nice to have company for once, and since I'm going to actually be at my apartment doing something other than sleeping tonight, stay and we'll catch up."

"We just hung out all day last weekend," I say, shaking my head at how quickly he seems to have forgotten the get-together at Grandma's just a week ago.

"Well, then we won't catch up. We can drink some beers and relax. After driving here at Mach two, I'd say you could use it."

It would be nice to drink a few beers and maybe have a few laughs with my brother. "Okay, sounds good. I'll meet you at your place."

"See you there!"

Alex walks away toward his car, leaving me wondering if maybe now's the time to finally tell someone in my family the truth of what I've been doing for the past two years. Maybe he'll have some ideas on how to break it to our mom and dad.

CHAPTER TEN

*S*avannah

THE PAST COUPLE DAYS HAVE PROVEN TO ME I HAVE no life. I do nothing. I roam around my house with little to do other than invent busy work to keep me occupied until I think of something else. It's not much of a life at all.

It does leave me with hours and hours of time to think, which isn't great either because all I can think about is Cash. Cheyenne's words about not getting attached to him echo in my mind over and over, but that only seems to make me fixate on him more.

He's someone who goes out with women in return for money. Why am I even bothering to remember his name, much less how beautiful his blue eyes are and how great he looked in that tux?

Not that I think his job is any less honorable than

any other one in the world. He helps out people who don't want to be stuck going to events like wedding receptions alone. It's actually quite admirable. To be a total stranger dropped into a family party like that and still have the ability to make a person feel better about themselves like Cash did for me isn't an easy task. Just dealing with my older sister probably made him think he should have charged double his usual rate.

Is it so wrong that I could find him physically and personally appealing?

I ask myself that as I pour myself a glass of red wine and wander back into the living room to sit there for a while. I spent two hours in the kitchen staring out at the gardens and wondering what he's doing today. Now I'll spend another couple in another room drinking and thinking about him.

Anyone who thinks this life is one they'd want hasn't lived like me for any real time. Yes, I want for nothing, but in needing nothing, I have nothing to do. If I had a job, I'd at least be able to occupy my time for eight hours a day with something other than thinking.

My husband used to tease me that my responsibilities as his wife were more taxing than his actual job running an entire company. The first time he said that I was sure he was simply being facetious. How could organizing caterers, landscapers, and a household staff around social events and parties meant to impress his friends and business associates be more difficult than a career as the CEO of an entire company?

I sigh and take a sip of my wine, loving the sweet

taste of it as it hits my tongue. What I'd give to have anything to plan, any occasion to celebrate right now.

Usually when I get like this, I call Cheyenne. Her life is the opposite of mine—always busy, filled with things to do and tasks to complete. She accomplishes so much every day, while I achieve nothing other than continuing to the next day.

The problem is I know what she'll say if I call her to talk about what's been on my mind since Saturday night. She's so level-headed, and before I can explain everything I've been thinking, she'll stop me with a sigh that tells me she thinks I'm being foolish or a shake of her head to let me know I'm not seeing things clearly.

Usually, I value that trait in her. It helps make decisions so much easier knowing she's by my side with her common sense attitude to support me when I begin to doubt myself.

Now, though, hearing her tsk-tsk or seeing her scowl when I say I had a good time and would like to hire him again would sting. Isn't it bad enough I've been alone for all this time? Can't I enjoy something without being told that I'm being ridiculous?

My phone rings on the table next to where I sit on the sofa, and I see my mother's name flash on the screen. I successfully avoided her for most of the wedding reception the other day, and the few moments when I had to deal with her, Cash stood by my side completely distracting her from her usual interrogation of me about everything from specifically why I haven't moved out of this house to in general when I planned to get on with my life.

Cecile comes by her brusque attitude naturally. So does my newly married brother. Where Cheyenne and I came from I have no idea. Perhaps it was the mailman. Twice. In the span of a couple years since we're two years apart.

Or did she have an ongoing affair with him that spanned many years? We do look like each other and not so much like our mother, father, or older siblings.

All of this runs through my mind at warp speed while my phone rings once, twice, and finally a third time before I answer it. I bet with other people when their mothers ask what took them so long to get to the phone, they can say they were lost in thought about who the real father of Cheyenne and me is. Not my mother. She wouldn't enjoy that tiny attempt at humor.

"Hi, Mom. What's new?" I ask, forcing myself to sound happier than I actually am.

"Savannah, I meant to call you yesterday, but your father and I were simply exhausted after the wedding and that lovely reception. Didn't you think it was gorgeous? Daria and her mother planned an utterly beautiful day for her and Spencer. He's so lucky to have met such a wonderful woman to be his wife."

My mother's way of speaking in glowing terms about everything regarding my new sister-in-law tells me she's trying too hard. I suspect if I push her even the tiniest bit, she'll go on and on for a half hour about whatever part of Saturday she didn't like. Was it the salmon entrée? She can be very difficult when it comes to that meal. Or maybe she thought the dancing portion of the reception went on too long. Since my father never did make it out onto the dance floor, I can see her complaining about that.

I don't want to encourage her to bash her only son's wedding day, though, so I agree with everything she says about Daria and the event and quickly move on to a different topic. "I loved your dress, Mom. I didn't realize when you told me it was a rose pink color how beautifully dusky that shade would be. You looked stunning."

"Oh, Savannah, thank you. I worried it was too young for a woman my age, but I'm happy to report that I got many compliments on it."

Diversion successful. Happy to have escaped the possible negativity that can envelope my mother far too often, I let her go on about her dress for a bit, pleased she felt so good in that very simple mother of the groom dress.

"As much as I could talk for hours about how I loved all the kind words I got on that dress, that's not what I called about. Your date for the wedding was all anyone could talk about, Savannah. He was literally all anyone could ask me about once they said how much they loved my dress. Everyone wants to know all about him. How long have you been dating? Where did you meet him? I told everyone that I had no idea, which made me look like some kind of negligent parent, of course, but I played it off as if I'd been so busy with wedding plans that I didn't pay attention when you told me every last detail about the young man. Cash is his name, right?"

While I should have expected the avalanche of questions from my family about Cash, I assumed I'd made it through the reception without having to answer too many and that would be that. How wrong I was, obviously.

Now that all the excitement of who's wearing what, who's drinking too much and making a fool of themselves, and who's offending which member of our family has died down, the attention has turned to my date for the day. Little do any of them know that's exactly the right way to say it.

"Yes, Mom. His name is Cash, but please don't make a big deal out of this. It's been hard enough getting back out there after all this time and after Carson's passing. Please understand I really don't want to talk about all the gory details regarding Cash and me."

I can't help but smile when I say that. Cash and me. There is no actual Cash and me in reality, but it's not like it's entirely impossible, is it? I'm an attractive young woman. He's a good looking man. We could get together and actually see one another, couldn't we?

Or maybe he doesn't do that.

Date, that is. Since he dates for a living, perhaps he doesn't want to do it in his time off. Or does he have someone already and he's not even single? That never occurred to me until this very moment. If that's the case, she's a lucky woman and very trusting. If he was my boyfriend, I wouldn't be okay with him escorting other women when he wasn't with me.

"Savannah Leigh, did you hear a word I just said?" my mother asks in exasperation.

Not having a clue what she's discussed with me in the time that my mind wandered off to Cash's possible relationship status, I have to admit I wasn't paying attention. Something my mother abhors.

"Sorry, Mom. I got distracted by a noise outside. What were you saying?" I say in my sweetest voice.

Normally, I don't prefer to lie, but to avoid the lecture about how it's rude to ignore people and how I should know better considering my age, something I've heard more than once in the recent past, I tell a tiny fib. It's better for her that I did that too. She doesn't need to get her blood pressure up, and I don't need to hear her give me chapter and verse on conversational etiquette.

"Is someone out there? I get nervous with you living in that big house all alone, Savannah. Why can't you convince Cheyenne to move back in with you? She's so headstrong, that one. Her date looked just like every man she's ever dated, I swear. Do you know what I thought as soon as I saw them walk up to the front door of the club? Gigolo. He looked like a gigolo. Tell me he didn't."

A laugh escapes from my throat at her use of that word to describe Nico. How ironic she isn't using it for Cash too. They were hired from the same service.

The same gigolo service.

"He seemed like a very nice person, Mom. We had a delightful discussion about 401Ks the other day."

My mother seizes on that tiny tidbit of information, much to my chagrin. "So is he a stockbroker or some kind of financial adviser? I asked your sister, but she said she was too busy to talk at the reception."

Damnit. I have no idea what Nico said he does when he isn't escorting women to family functions they don't want to be caught dead at alone.

"I think so, but I don't know. There was so much going on that day, so I don't want to say definitely."

"So what's happening with this man of yours? Tell me."

"He's very nice, but I don't want to jinx anything, Mom, so for now, let's just say I like him."

My mother immediately responds like I knew she would at the mention of that word jinx. A superstitious person, she believes in bad omens and bringing bad luck on yourself is a real thing. While I may not put any stock in all of that, I know simply bringing it up will allow me to be vague and escape this conversation.

"Oh, then of course, we'll table this discussion for another day. I do want you to know that I liked him a lot. He's very handsome, very personable, and obviously quite bright. What does he do again?"

That question I can answer. "He owns a restaurant."

"Ooooh, a restauranteur. I like the sound of that.

My daughter Savannah and her boyfriend the restauranteur."

"It's restaurateur, Mom. No n."

And with that little correction, my mother says, "Savannah, your father is calling me, so I better go. Tell Cheyenne she needs to call me. I want to know more about this Nico person."

"Okay, Mom. I'll tell her."

In the background, I hear my father bellow my mother's name, so she quickly says, "Okay, bye dear."

And with that, I can safely say I don't have to answer any questions about Cash for the near future. My sister isn't going to be so lucky, though.

CHEYENNE FINISHES HER FIRST GLASS OF WINE AND pours a second one, already needing more alcohol after I told her about our mother's planned grilling of her about Nico. "Isn't it enough to just see a gorgeous man with me and think, 'Good for my daughter?' Why does Mom have to make this something it isn't?"

"Because she spends her time worrying about the two of us becoming spinsters."

My sister nearly spits out her mouthful of wine. "First of all, it's the twenty-first century, for God's sake. That isn't a thing anymore. If I never want to get married, so be it. Second, you can't be a spinster, technically according to her old fashioned rules, because you already got married, so you're safe. I, on the other hand, am in grave danger of never meeting

Mr. Right and being far too happy settling for Mr. Right Now."

That joke hits a little too close to home for me, and I quickly turn away, knowing that if she sees the look in my eyes at this moment, she'll know that I've been spending the last two days thinking of Cash. The problem is my sister catches my attempt to avoid her gaze and immediately jumps on it.

"Let me guess. You didn't take my advice about him, and now you're thinking you want to see him again, right?" she asks with far too much judgment.

"Please don't make this something I should feel bad about," I say quietly, focusing on the wine in my glass instead of facing her. "It's not a crime to like someone, Cheyenne."

"No one ever said it was a crime. Foolish, yes. Crime, no. So you've been pining away since he dropped you off Saturday night. Did you call the service to arrange something?"

I snap my head around to look at her standing near the kitchen window, hating how she phrased that. Pining away sounds so nineteenth century, like some Jane Austen sad heroine.

"Nobody's been pining away. Do you have to be so mean?"

"Well, you know what you have to do. You have to call."

She says that like she has to twist my arm to spend more time with Cash. I like him. It's not like it would be a punishment.

Marching over to where I sit at the kitchen table,

she picks up my phone and holds it in front of my face. "Call and ask directly for him alone. That will give you your answer."

"What do you mean?" I ask, suddenly terrified of the phone two inches away from my nose.

"If he declines the job, that's your answer. Not that I think if he does decide to go out with you again that it means he likes you the way you do him. He's a man who's paid to go out with women, Savannah. That's what he does. I told you not to get attached, but you didn't listen, so you have to call and ask for him directly. That will tell you everything you need to know."

Hurt by how brusque she's being with my feelings, I push her hand away to get that damn phone out of my face. "Stop talking to me like I don't know all of this. You sound like Cecile when you get like that."

"Like what? Honest?"

Her expression says she thinks I'm a fool, and I don't know what hurts more—that she thinks that about me or that Cash might not even care one tiny bit about me when I can't stop thinking of him after only one date.

God, maybe I am just a fool.

"Just go, Cheyenne. Forget I said anything, okay? Just leave me alone."

"Don't be like that, Savannah. Love takes guts, so just make the call. I'll be right here for moral support."

I look at her to see if she intended to sound so sarcastic. She doesn't seem to be wearing her snotty face she usually has on when she's being snide.

"This isn't love, so stop acting like that. I just liked being around him."

Cheyenne shrugs, like all of this is crazy to her. "Fine, it's not about love. Whatever it's about, make the call. Bite the bullet. Grab the bull by the horns."

"I know you're trying to be supportive, but can you tone it down a little? You sound like some practically rabid football coach. I'm getting cold feet about this whole thing with you talking about it like that."

Holding my phone out in front of me again, she smiles. "Just make the call."

My hand shaking, I take it and dial the number for the service where he works. This is crazy. No wonder my sister was looking at me like she thinks I'm nuts.

I listen to the voice prompts, giving my name and number, and when it comes time to include any specific requests, I swallow hard and hope that I can get the words out. All I have to do is say his name and that I would like to book him again. Just a few simple words and then I can hang up.

Cheyenne waves her hands like she's trying to land a jet on the deck of a ship, and I finally choke out the words. "I'd like to have Cash again, please."

Suddenly panicked, I end the call and toss my cell phone onto the table. I did it. I made the call and asked to see him again.

My sister pours me another glass of much-needed wine and raises her glass to toast me. "I love how you said you wanted to have him again. Perfect phrasing!"

Oh, God! I said I wanted to have Cash again, like

I'd already had him in that way. I don't even know the person who listens to those messages, but I'm completely mortified.

Burying my face in my hands, I shake my head in disbelief. "I can't believe I said it like that."

Cheyenne laughs at my misery. "By the way, I bet that bull has a nice horn. I can't wait to hear if I'm right."

And now my mortification is complete.

ash

MY BROTHER SITS ACROSS FROM ME IN HIS LIVING room, the two of us enjoying a beer after the day we had at the hospital. Well, more than a single beer. One beer wouldn't be enough. Not for me, at least.

Every time I see my mother in that bed, even if she's able to get up and walk around whenever she wants to, it's like someone dropping a hundred pound weight on my chest. That's why I'm on my fifth and plan to keep drinking until I can't think anymore.

"Try the egg rolls. They're made with steak and imported provolone cheese," Alex proudly says as he pushes the plate full of them toward me across the coffee table.

I grab one and bite into it. Like with everything he makes, it's incredible.

"How do you do it? The last thing I want to do is make anything to eat after today. I swear to God if they don't let her out soon, I'm going to lose it."

He takes a drink of his beer and shrugs. "This is how I handle things. Making food helps me think about something that I find happiness in, so it's the first thing I turn to when I have to deal with something like what's happening to Mom."

"Seems completely sane and healthy to me," I say with a chuckle. "Are you sure you're actually a March?"

My joke makes him smile, and he reaches over the table to get an egg roll. "Pretty sure, although I still can't believe how often I get confused with being not Dad's kid but Stefan's. Any chance Mom and our uncle had a wild night twenty-four years ago and nobody's come clean?"

For a long moment, I try to imagine our mother with Stefan. Nope. Doesn't work. He's not serious enough for her.

"I'm not seeing that. Now if you said Kane, I'd be able to entertain that idea more, as far as uncles go. But not Stefan."

"Must just be some kind of super transferable gene thing Grandma, Stefan, Cade, and I have then."

I nod, trying to think if anyone else in our family has that dark hair and brown eyes thing going on. Oh, yeah. One more. "Don't forget Ava. She must have gotten that super transferable gene too."

Alex shakes his head. "Nah, she looks like Shay, though. I think it's just the three of us. Weird, don't you think? I mean, Mom's got brown eyes, but look at you. You're the spitting image of Dad, and while I look a little like her, I look way more like Stefan and Cade."

Raising my beer bottle in the air, I make a toast. "Thanks to the amazing and bizarre world of genetics, we all look like either Dad or Stefan. Even the ones who aren't actually blood related to us."

After I take a sip of my beer to celebrate that idea that in my quasi-drunken mind sounds pretty damn interesting, I ask, "Wilder get himself straightened out yet, or is he still more fucked up than anyone wants to admit?"

Our cousin is always a sore spot in any family discussion, even with Alex, who tends to simply let most things roll off his back like water off a duck. He twists his expression into a grimace at my mention of Wilder and says, "I'll go with more fucked up than anyone wants to admit. I haven't spent any real time with him recently. Hell, it's been years, if I'm being honest, and I don't have a problem with that. After he and Cade got into it a few months ago, he stopped coming by the restaurant. Count me as someone who thinks that's a good idea."

"You think he's still fucked up because he went to jail?" I ask, suddenly curious about that since I rarely even see Wilder anymore.

Alex shakes his head. "I have no idea. Cade thinks his whole thing is just a ploy to get sympathy."

My brother's always been closer to Cade than he has with me. I used to hate that. I'd be so jealous when

Stefan and Shay sent him over to spend the weekend or when he'd come on vacations with us. Alex and Cade looked like brothers while I got to look like the rest of the family. I wanted Alex to be happy to hang out with me, but it was never like that with us.

For a long time, I blamed Cade. In my mind, if only he didn't exist, then Alex and I would be best friends like those two were. That wasn't how it would ever be, though. I love my brother, but we're like night and day.

Still, he's the only one I have, so while I may not understand him or why he does the things he does most of the time, I try to do whatever I can to stay close with him. Not that he gets how I am either. He thinks I'm this uptight, always do the right thing kind of person, and compared to his laid back approach with its focus on enjoying life as much as you can, my outlook looks entirely too restricted to him.

Alex would never consider being a lawyer in a million years. It possesses no charm, no creativity for him. So that's how he sees me.

But I wonder if he knew the truth if he'd still consider me as boring as he's always thought.

Maybe it's the alcohol or maybe it's just that I'm tired of carrying around the truth and not having anyone to talk to about it, other than Damon, but when I finish my beer, I sit back against the couch and look across the room at my brother as I think of how I want to tell him what I've really been doing for the past two years. Any way is going to surprise him, but I want this to come out right when I finally say it.

Clearing my throat, I decide on how to approach the subject and take a deep breath in. "You know that graduation party Mom is so excited about?"

He nods and lifts the bottle to his lips to finish his beer. "Yeah. I'm thinking she's planning on inviting every person she's ever met. I'm talking the woman at the grocery store who told her she liked her hair five years ago, the guy who runs the dry cleaners she sometimes uses when she doesn't go with the one closer to the house, and every parent from high school whose kid graduated with us."

I empty the air out of my lungs is a loud whoosh. "Yeah, well, she's not going to have to."

Alex's expression turns dark, and he angrily snaps, "Cash, don't be an asshole. Mom's going to be fine. Fuck, man. You get fucking dark when you drink. You know that? I think I'm going to go to bed. Eat the rest of the damn egg rolls, if you want."

He moves to get up, but I quickly sit up straight on the sofa and put my hand up to stop him. "Alex, that's not what I meant. Sit down. Please. I'm talking about something else, and I need to get this off my chest, okay?"

For a few seconds, he looks like he's trying to decide between doing what I ask and punching me. Far more physical than I am, there's every chance he might do both he looks so pissed right now.

"Fine, but this better be something good because right now I think I want to beat the hell out of you for making it sound like Mom isn't going to be around for your graduation."

So far, this is going as badly as it could. Let's hope when I tell him the truth about who I really am and what I've been up to all this time that I've been up in Gainesville that he won't react even worse.

"I'd never say that, Alex. Just hear me out because I need to tell someone or I don't know what I'm going to do."

Narrowing his eyes to slits, he stares at me like he's confused now. Talk about a rollercoaster of emotions. One minute he's ready to fight me and the next he can't figure out what the hell I'm talking about.

"Okay. Now I'm thinking you're about to come out to me. Is that what this is? Because it's cool and all, but I have to say I didn't see this coming," he says with a fair amount of resignation.

Nice. Now my entire sexuality is what he thinks I'm talking about. Christ, could this get worse?

"First of all, no. Why would you think I was gay?" I ask, happy to divert from my intended points for a few minutes.

He shrugs like it isn't anything he's put much thought into. "You don't really have a lot of girlfriends. You never have. Maybe that's because you're into guys."

"As a matter of fact, I have someone I just met who I'm thinking maybe something could happen with, so no, I'm not into guys. You know, Liam has never had a lot of girlfriends either. And I'm not sure I've ever seen Wilder with a woman. Do you think they're gay too?"

"Now that you bring it up," he says with a chuckle, giving me yet another shrug.

"Well, I don't know if Wilder is, but Liam isn't and neither am I. You know, just because we're not manwhores like you and Cade doesn't mean we don't like women. Maybe we're just too busy."

That gets me a big smile. "Not that I'm not enjoying this roundabout discussion and attack on my sex life, but what the hell are you trying to say here, Cash?"

My heart races as I formulate the words in my brain. I just need to say them once and for all and tell someone so I don't have to carry this around alone any longer.

Looking down at the beer bottle in my hand, I finally tell someone the truth. "There won't be a graduation, so there's no need for Mom to plan a graduation party."

I hear nothing after my confession. My brother doesn't say a word, and I swear I can't even hear him breathing. In fact, the only sound I hear after a few seconds is my heartbeat pounding in my ears.

The truth is supposed to set you free. Isn't that what they always say? At least someone said it before. But I don't feel freer after finally saying those words. Maybe it's because that wasn't the entire truth.

Lifting my head, I see Alex staring at me in astonishment. Stunned, like some deer in the headlights unable to move as a car comes barreling down the road toward them. I don't think I've ever seen him react this way about anything.

When he doesn't say a word or ask why there won't be a graduation, I say, "I'm not graduating because I haven't been in law school for two years. I dropped out in my first year and never went back."

That piece of news makes his mouth drop open and his eyes grow even wider. I'm halfway there, and to be honest, I'd expected Alex to accept this news a bit more casually. If the most relaxed person I know is reacting this way, I can only imagine what it will be like when I tell my mother and father.

After nearly a minute of silence and staring in shock at me, he finally asks the question I expected. "So what the hell have you been doing up there this whole time?"

This is the part that's going to be the most difficult to explain. It's one thing that I dropped out of law school and lied to everyone for years about it. That's bad enough. Having to admit I've been running a business that may or may not walk the finest of lines between legal and criminal is so much harder.

There's no turning back now. I wanted to unburden myself of this entire story, and I can't stop two-thirds of the way through.

"I run a company with a friend of mine from law school. He dropped out too. We make a lot of money helping people out when they need someone to escort them to events."

That may be the most clinical way I've ever thought about what Damon and I do for a living. I could have just said we run an escort service, but something in me wanted to make it sound less like it actually is and more professional.

None of it fools Alex, though. "So you and your

friend hire women to escort men to events? I think that's called being a pimp, Cash."

So much for sounding professional.

"Not women. Only men."

"Are we back to the gay thing again?"

I can't help roll my eyes. "No, we're not. We have guys who escort women to things like wedding receptions and charity functions. It's entirely asexual, so it's not pimping anything."

My brother makes a face like he's trying to figure out what all of this means. "So, entirely asexual means you don't just have good looking guys who go with older women and then fuck them. Am I getting this right?"

Jesus, when I hear it said like that, it does sound bad.

Waving my hands in front of me, I try to stop him from continuing along that line of thought. "No, no. You're looking at this all wrong. Let me explain how it all started. A friend of ours in law school needed someone to take her to this thing with her family. She didn't want to go alone. You can understand that. Going to family functions when everyone else is married sucks, and from every woman I've ever talked to about it, going as a single woman sucks ten times as much. So we helped her out so she didn't have to suffer through it alone. Nothing big, but she was so thankful she gave us a few bucks. Damon and I weren't happy doing the whole law school thing anyway, so when we realized this could be something we could make money at, we started our business."

"What's the name?" Alex asks.

"The name?"

"Yeah. It's a business, so it has to have a name, right?"

The memory of Damon and me joking about what to call the escort business that night we decided to make a go of it flashes through my mind, and I chuckle. "Well, we considered calling it The Meat Market, but that sounded a little obvious. It doesn't have a name, technically. It's just a number that some women have, and if they like the service, they give the number to their friends."

My answer doesn't seem to please him. At least it doesn't look like it by the scowl he gives me.

"Okay, so it doesn't have a name, so it's not paying taxes on the money you two make. I might be a lowly chef, but that sounds illegal."

"Well…"

I really didn't want to get into all these details, but I should have known Alex would zero in on them. He's not lowly in any sense of the word, and although he didn't spend as much time in school as I have, little gets by him.

But he quickly moves from the tax issues to other, more obvious, ones.

"I'm not lawyer, Cash, and obviously, you aren't going to be either, it seems, but this sounds an awful lot like you getting paid to have people get together. Isn't that illegal? I mean, this is Florida, so who knows, but is it legal?"

Now that's the question of the year. Damon and I

set up the business assuming we might someday get into a bit of hot water if anyone ever claimed we were selling sex. That's why the bank accounts are all offshore and the payments go through cryptocurrency. It's also why no one knows we're the two people behind the business.

"Yes and no," I answer honestly, not really interested in getting into the legal intricacies of how fine that line is we walk every day.

My brother sits back hard in his chair, clearly stunned at all he's heard. Once and then twice he opens his mouth to say something, but no words come out.

Finally, he blows the air out of his mouth like all of this has exhausted him. "Cash, you need to tell Mom and Dad. Maybe not about this business you've got, but you have to tell them the truth about law school. Mom's been running around town planning this party with Grandma like it's a goddamned coronation for you."

Nodding, I say, "I know. Last weekend, I wanted to hide every time she brought that subject up. I even tried today when you and Dad went down to the hospital cafeteria for coffee. I couldn't bring myself to do it."

"Well, maybe now's not exactly the right time, but you have to do it in the next few months."

Hanging my head, I stare down at the floor and wish more than anything I could find a way out of doing that. "It's going to break her heart, Alex. Dad's too, but she's been so invested in the idea that I'm going to be a lawyer. She's going to be so disappointed."

God, I hate that the most. My father will take it like he's always taken bad news. He'll nod and probably say I should have told him, but that will be about it. My mother will unravel. I'll see that look in her eyes, the one that shows she's hurt, and I'll be the one who put that look in them once again. That's going to kill me to see that.

"Cash, listen to me. No matter what you do, you could never disappoint Mom."

I lift my head to see him smiling at me. "You underestimate my ability to fail, baby brother."

He shakes his head, like he can't believe that. "She loves you. How many times has she told the story of how you were her miracle baby? The one she never thought she could have. She won't be disappointed like you think, but the longer you let this go, the harder it's going to be."

"That's just it, though. Her miracle baby was supposed to grow up to be what she wanted. But he didn't."

"She wanted you to be a lawyer because she thought you wanted that. We all did. I had no idea you didn't love law school. You seemed happy all this time. You just need to let this whole health scare blow over and then you have to tell them."

"I know. I will. I'll do it. I just need to find the right moment."

Alex stands up and takes the beer bottle out of my hand. "At least I know why you were pounding them down tonight. Don't worry. Mom will be fine with everything."

He leaves me alone with my thoughts, but the truth is, it's not just my mother's hospital stay or the lie I'm living that's on my mind tonight. Savannah's in the mix too. I swore I'd never let myself feel anything for the women I do jobs for. It's one of the reasons why I don't like taking them anymore if I can help it.

I couldn't help it this time, though, and now I'm wondering what to do with the fact that I can't stop thinking of her. Yet another woman I've been lying to.

Maybe I would have made a good lawyer.

ash

WE WAIT FOR MY PARENTS AT THEIR HOUSE AFTER the hospital released my mother early this morning, and after making sure that she's okay, I return to living my lie and telling them I have to get back to Gainesville so I don't miss any more classes. Every word tastes like ash in my mouth when I say them this time, even though I've told that exact lie more times than I can count in the past two years.

"Oh, honey, you get back to school where you belong. You didn't have to stay until they let me go. You've been here since Saturday night, so you've missed not only Monday classes but today's too," my mother says sweetly, making my guilt multiply exponentially.

"It's no problem, Mom. I wanted to be here.

Anything that's happening back there can wait. You're more important."

She takes my face in her hands and stares up at me like I'm the most precious thing in the world to her. "You are such a good son, Cash. Thank you for staying, but I'm in good hands with your father and your brother. Go back and do your schoolwork."

"Okay, Mom. I love you. I'll be back maybe this weekend to check up on you, okay?"

"Only if it doesn't get in the way of an exam or anything important with school."

"It won't. I promise."

Alex gives me a sideways glance when he hears me say that, and on my way out, he catches me near the front door. My brother can be trusted to keep my secret, but I doubt he wants to be the only one in on it for much longer.

"Don't worry about Mom. I'd say you have other things to deal with. Do you know when you're going to tell them?" he asks as we walk out to my car.

"I have a few months, I think. I don't want to upset her while she's still under the weather."

My brother practically bores a hole through me with his direct look after I say that. "I get it, but a few months might be too long to wait. She's going to be putting down deposits on all sorts of things from caterers to designers to handle the party, so I'd say do it before the holidays."

I stop and open my car door, eager to leave if only to get some reprieve from the reality of what I need to do and soon. "Okay. You're right. If she's feeling better by the end of this month, I'll do it then."

"Good. The longer this goes on, the harder it will be, Cash. It's like a Band-Aid. You just have to rip it off."

"That's the second time this week someone's said that to me. I'm starting to see a theme here," I say with a laugh.

"I thought I was the only one who knew, other than your business partner," Alex says, confused and probably thinking I messed up my story since I was so drunk last night.

"No, he said it about Emily, that girl I was seeing. She keeps messaging me, wanting to get back together, and I keep avoiding her," I explain as I get in behind the wheel.

Alex nods, giving me a knowing smile. "I think you're right. There is a theme there. It's called avoidance."

"And you'd never have that problem, of course," I say, rolling my eyes.

His smile grows to a broad grin. Opening his arms wide, he tilts his head back and laughs. "I avoid nothing. Good, bad, whatever, I'm take it all in. You should try it sometime."

"See you later, Alex. Call me if anything happens."

As I back the car up to leave, I study my brother standing there reveling in the sun shining down on him. He'd be perfect to work for Damon and me. Good looking, fun, smart, and a great cook, women would fall over themselves to hire him to escort them around town.

Then again, he already has a life he's happy with. If I'm going to find new guys so I don't have to do any more weddings, it's not going to be with family members.

~

WHILE I DRIVE BACK TO MY CONDO AT A MUCH slower speed than on my way to Tampa, I give Damon a call to check on how everything went over the weekend. Holidays are always busy, and from what he said, September is going to be the big month to get married, so I figure we're about to be up to our eyes in requests, if we aren't already.

"Hey, Cash, what's up? How's your mom doing? I hope it's good news."

"Yeah, she's doing much better. Thanks. They think they got the situation under control with meds, but they're going to keep it under observation for a while. You know how the heart is. You don't want to fuck around with it," I explain, choosing to be intentionally vague with him since I'm not really up to discussing all that's happened.

Music in the background begins to drown him out as he begins to speak, so he says, "Hang on. I need to go out on the balcony."

"Sounds like a good time. You having a party?" I ask, curious since Damon is more of the kind of guy who prefers to hang out with a few people, get drunk, and yell at the TV and whatever game he's watching.

He doesn't answer for a few seconds, and then I hear a door close and the music disappears. "Not me. Ashley. She asked a couple of her friends and their boyfriends over. I'm in fucking hell, Cash. Like literally in hell. The devil is looking at what I'm dealing with here tonight and thinking to himself, 'Damn, that guy deserves a break.' It's that bad. I'm pretty sure I'm not going to make it through the night."

I can't help but laugh at how overwrought he sounds because of a little party that girlfriend of his forced on him. "She's making you the host with the most, isn't she? If you don't like having them all there in your apartment, send them home. It is your place."

"Spoken like a true single guy. I want to be you when I grow up, you know that?"

"You were me until a few months ago, man. You're not married to Ashley. You can be single again tonight if you toss all those people out and send her with them."

Damon makes a groaning noise like he's trying to decide if he should stay with his girlfriend or break up with her and some part of him has already chosen to keep her around. He's never said anything about why he keeps dating her, but I'm guessing the part that likes her the most is between his legs.

"I better get back in there before she starts making decisions about what to do with my TV, but I haven't checked the messages since Sunday night. Sorry about that, but Ashley has me running around like a chicken with my head cut off these past few days and I slacked off."

Great. Unlike Damon's dick, I'm not a fan of Ashley, and her way of making him forget he's running a business with me that needs tending every damn day pisses me off. After the few days I've had, I'm emotionally wrung out and my first reaction to his slacking is to lash out at him.

But there's no point in that, so I take a deep breath in, switch lanes to get past the truck in front of me that can't seem to get up to speed to be on this damn road, and sigh. "No problem. I'll check them on my way. I'm not doing anything else, so it'll keep my focus because I'm beat."

"Thanks, Cash. I appreciate you not reaming me out for being such a shithead lately. I swear things will even out soon. Either she'll go, or I'll figure out a way to work and be with her."

I tell him it's fine, even though it's not, but all I can think is that's just about the lamest explanation of how a relationship is working that I've ever heard. Definitely not anything I'd want in my life.

The miles fly past as I listen to message after message, saving all of them to deal with tomorrow morning. Whoever wrote that article Damon read about September being the new popular month for weddings knew what they were talking about. Woman after woman after woman needing someone to be her plus one at all their friends' and families' weddings. Well, that's what we're here for, so tomorrow morning

I'll get on each and every one of them to ensure our customers get what they want.

When I'm just about home, I hear a voice I recognize immediately. Savannah says her name and number, and then as I wait to know what she needs another escort for, she says she wants me again.

The message says it came in yesterday, Monday afternoon. Thanks, Damon.

Then again, I can't say I'm unhappy about him not knowing she requested to see me a second time. I have no interest in explaining anything to him about Savannah.

Even as I don't exactly know what I'd say if anyone asked what's going on. She was sweet and I had a good time talking to her. The rest of the reception was as bad as wedding receptions usually go, but when I think of Savannah, I smile.

That doesn't mean I necessarily should see her again. The sound of her voice gives me the hint she's already far more attached than she should be, and as much as she's been on my mind, I'm not looking for anything serious with anyone.

Other than the fact that it's full of lies, I like my life as it is. Single, without a woman inviting people over to my place and making me wish I could escape.

All of this runs through my head as I drive toward her house, my subconscious clearly more interested in seeing her than I thought. She was sweet, and it could be nice to talk to someone after the last few days. In fact, the idea of sitting alone in my place staring at some ballgame on TV as I replay everything regarding my mother sounds like the last thing I want to do tonight.

Even though she left her number, I drive directly to her house without calling first. It's presumptuous and probably rude, but she wanted to see me again.

I wait at the front door after ringing the bell, and when the door opens and I see her standing there in a pair of black shorts and a green t-shirt, I suddenly don't know what to say. I didn't exactly think this thing through before showing up here, and now that she's in front of me looking not like some wealthy woman in need of a date for a wedding but a woman I would be interested in, I'm tongue-tied.

Savannah looks down her body and then back up at me in horror. "Cash, what are you doing here?"

"I got your message."

Tucking her long brown hair behind her ear, she looks away, but I see her cheeks turn pink from a blush. "Oh. I thought since I never heard back that you weren't interested in seeing me again."

I wasn't wrong about what I heard in her voice in that message. She's already too interested in me. She wouldn't be embarrassed at being so thrilled to see me if she wasn't. I should turn around and leave right now. This is a mistake.

"Maybe I should leave. I didn't call, so this shouldn't happen," I mumble, unsure what to do but not wanting to go.

"You can come in, if you want," she says quietly. "Are you okay? You look like something's wrong. Not that I really know you, but I know the universal sign for something's not right."

I look back at her and shake my head. "What's that?"

Pointing at my face, she says, "The frown. Unless it's me because I'm wearing these clothes. They aren't what people usually see me in."

Now her expression turns sad to match mine, so I quickly say, "You look great. I've just had a bad few days, but I doubt you want to hear about that. I should go."

Her hand gently touches my forearm, and I look down at the spot where her fingers rest against my skin and then up at her. In her eyes, I see something gentle and sweet I want right now.

More than want. Need.

CHAPTER THIRTEEN

ash

"IF YOU WANT TO COME IN AND TALK, I'LL LISTEN."

I don't know why, but something about those two simple words—I'll listen—makes me smile, so when she steps back from the door, I walk into the house. I instantly see that the gorgeous outside doesn't do the inside justice. The spacious foyer I step into is all white and soars to at least twenty feet high. Above my head, a pair of enormous wrought iron light fixtures shaped like inverted bells hang on either side of the space. I look down to see white marble below my feet that meets up with a dark wood floor at the foyer's entrances to what look like a dining room, a living room, and another room I can't figure out yet.

"Your house is breathtaking," I say, suddenly feeling out of place.

My family has always had money. My grandparents were wealthy, and my parents' generation only increased the amount of money the March family possesses.

But compared to Savannah, we have nothing.

"Thank you. It's very big and I live here alone, so to me it feels more like a museum than a home. There are some rooms I haven't been in this year."

She stops for a moment and I see she's uncomfortable when she adds, "To be honest, this isn't the kind of home for one person. It's too much."

"Do you like it?"

Savannah thinks about that question for a long time as we stand there in her stunning foyer and finally says, "I wish I liked it more than I do. Would you like to sit down?"

I nod and follow her toward the doorway straight ahead I guessed led to a living room. Another enormous space, this room has floor-to-ceiling windows that look out onto the pool area outside and at this time of day offer a view of the night sky I would have thought could only be seen from somewhere in the country, off in the middle of nowhere without any interference from city lights.

Walking over to look out, I stand there in awe of the beauty she has right outside her windows to enjoy any time she likes. "This is a stunning view. It's like you can see every star there is in the heavens."

She joins me and looks up, but the way she narrows her eyes and sighs, I get the sense she doesn't appreciate it as much as I do. Or maybe it's just that it's so commonplace for her while it's extraordinary for me.

"When my sister lived here, we'd go swimming and have parties out there all the time. I can't remember the last time I stepped foot in that pool, though."

The sadness in her voice only serves to amplify mine that's been building for the past few days because of my mother. Maybe this wasn't a good idea after all. Two sad people aren't going to do each other any good. Then again, misery does love company, or at least that's what they always say.

"Would you like something to drink?" she asks next to me as I continue to gaze out those windows to the view that makes me feel so insignificant at this moment.

"Just some water, actually. It was a long drive back from Tampa tonight, and I'm suddenly parched."

"Okay. Would you like to see the kitchen? We can sit in there and talk, if you like. It's not as cavernous as this room too, so I like to spend time in there when people come over."

I follow her again, this time through a series of rooms that flow one from the other. What looks like a second living room, this one with a huge seventy inch TV, the dining room I saw from the foyer before, and finally into the kitchen. Her home reminds me of that time when my mother decided she wanted to buy new furniture for our house when I was a little boy and she dragged me from showroom to showroom looking for exactly the pieces she wanted. Room after room of furniture ran into one another, each one perfectly placed and looking like no one had ever sat on any piece even once.

The kitchen, like all of the house I've seen so far, is white, but looking down, I see a floor of tan and white marble mixed with a lighter wood over near a little nook where a round table sits surrounded by windows. She points me toward that spot as she heads toward the refrigerator on the other side of the room.

"Make yourself comfortable while I get us some water."

That little nook seems so out of place with the rest of the house, and when I sit down, I look out the window to see a tiny garden. This view offers no expansive sky full of stars or a vista in the distance. Just that area full of what seem to be wildflowers.

Savannah places a tall glass of water in front of me on the wood table and sits down in the chair nearest to me and the windows. Looking out, she points toward the flowers and says, "Those are mine. Everything else the gardeners and landscapers handle, but that little patch of yard is all mine. I planted the flowers and I take care of them. I think the landscaper thinks I'm insane because they're just ordinary flowers. He's always talking about how this or that would look perfect there for me to see when I'm sitting here, but I want these flowers. I see the gardener skulking around them sometimes, looking at them like they're weeds or something. I think they're beautiful."

"I do too," I say, liking the idea that there's something at this place that's like her.

Turning around, she sets her glass of water on the

table and smiles at me. "Your family lives in Tampa. I remember you saying something about that at the wedding."

"Yeah. My parents and all my family are back there. That's who I went to see right after I dropped you off that night. My mother was rushed to the hospital after my father found her unconscious on the floor at their house."

Even now, saying those words makes my chest get tight. Savannah reaches over and touches my hand to give it a gentle squeeze, and I'm surprised at how much better that makes me feel.

"Is she going to be okay?" she asks in a tentative voice, probably afraid the next thing I'm going to say will be even worse.

I nod and let out a heavy sigh I think I might have been holding in since Alex called me Saturday night. "The doctors say she's going to be fine now. They have her on the right medication, so things look good. I don't know why the whole thing hit me so hard. My mother's tough. I should have known she'd come through it fine."

As I make my excuse for why I feel so torn up about everything that's happened in the past few days, Savannah simply shakes her head. "It's okay to admit your mother being sick makes you upset. When someone you love is suddenly in danger, it's only right that you're emotionally affected. Even cool guys like you have license to feel when your mother is sick. I'm just glad she's going to be okay."

"Cool guys like me?" I ask with a smile. "So I'm a cool guy?"

Not that I don't know this already. All my life I've been that person. Calm, cool, collected. Very much like my father. While my mother and Alex are always showing how they feel, my father and I are as cool as cucumbers, as she likes to say.

"I didn't have to spend more than a few minutes around you to figure that out," Savannah says with a cute chuckle. "You look cool, and when you speak, you're very calm and composed. People like me always wish we could be like you are. Nothing ruffles you, I bet, which is why this scare with your mother frightened you so much."

She strangely seems to know just how I feel, which is odd since we barely know one another. Still, it's nice to be able to talk to someone and not think I have to be anything but that scared son I was and tried to hide since Saturday.

"It did scare me. My mother's a great person. She's what my grandmother calls a spitfire. She can be sweet and nice one minute, but then you get her ire up, and she's a redheaded force of nature. I can't imagine her not being around, which I know probably sounds ridiculous since I know she's not eternal. I'm just not ready to lose her yet."

I have to look away as I confess that because if I don't, I think I might tear up. The thought of losing my mother is too much to bear. I always thought I'd have more time. She's never seen me do much of anything, and even though I don't want to be that lawyer she thinks I do, I wanted her to see me get married some day and give her grandchildren.

"You're never ready to lose the people you love, Cash," she says, and I hear the genuine compassion of someone who's been through losing someone in her voice.

Looking at her, I smile. "I'm supposed to be the cool guy, but for the past few days, I've been a mess. How did you do it and come through to be able to talk about it?"

I don't say losing her husband because it feels like intruding. She gets to say those words, not me. That's her pain, and she has the right to talk about it any way she wants. I didn't understand that until I had to grapple with how much it hurt to see my mother lying in that hospital bed.

"By the way I can talk about it now, you might think I was all strength and understanding when I lost Carson. I wasn't. I think I sort of had it better than many people who lose someone they love, though. I knew for a while he was dying. He did too, so we just made sure to spend every minute we could enjoying life. I can only imagine if it had been a surprise after having him in my life for twenty years. I don't think I would have been able to handle it, to be honest. He gets most of the credit, though."

Surprised, I ask, "For what?"

"For making it bearable. It's always hard. Death is never something anyone handles easily, but Carson made it possible for me to endure the pain."

"How?"

She thinks about my question for a moment and says, "He did everything he could to make me feel like I didn't miss anything with him. We were only married for two years, but he packed a lifetime of memories into that time. Then, when it became clear that there was nothing else to be done and the cancer wasn't going to go away, he arranged everything so I'd never have to do without again. That's the kind of person he was. Emotions were good, but practical measures were what he thought showed people he truly cared about them."

"He sounds like a great guy."

A big smile lights up her face. "He was. He used to joke when we first met that I was going to outlive him, and when he got sick, he'd say, 'See? I knew it from the moment I saw you that you'd outlast me.' I never cared about him being so much older than I was, though. Others may have, but I don't look at people and see age."

My curiosity about how old her husband was makes me forget my manners, and I ask, "How much older than you was he?"

The words barely make it out of my mouth before I wish I hadn't said them. "I'm sorry. That was rude. I think I'll just go now."

But she shakes her head and tightens her hold on my hand, as if she wants to make sure I don't leave yet. "No, it's fine," she says with a sweet smile. "Carson was fifty when we married, and I was twenty-five. In my defense, I don't think I have a daddy thing so much as a powerful guy thing. Plus, he didn't look that old. Here, let me show you a picture of him."

She scrolls through her pictures on her phone until she finds the one she's looking for and turns it so the screen is facing me. "That was right after we got married. We'd just gotten back from our honeymoon. See? It wasn't like he looked like Methuselah. Anyway, age is just a number."

I study the picture of her husband from those days when they were so happy, and I have to admit he doesn't look like a man in his fifties then. Maybe early forties, and even at that age, he looked great. I can definitely see why a beautiful young woman would like him, especially considering how wealthy he was.

"He looks happy. That's a good thing for you to have to remember him by."

Savannah turns the phone back toward her and runs her finger over the screen. "Even then, he was sick and we didn't even know it. Never forget sunscreen, Cash. It sounds like a silly thing to say to another adult, but don't forget it. Skin cancer can kill, and it's just like any other disease. It takes people you love and you can't get them back."

"I'm sorry. I didn't mean to upset you. I shouldn't have come here tonight. I'm a mess of emotions I don't know what to do with, and now you're the one who has to deal with them. That's not fair."

When I get up to go, Savannah stops me. "Please don't. Stay. It's okay. Honest."

Even though I know I shouldn't, I don't want to leave.

CHAPTER FOURTEEN

*S*avannah

MY EMOTIONS GET ALL JUMBLED AS I TALK TO CASH about the life I used to have. It's been two years. I should be able to talk about Carson and all that happened then without tearing up.

No wonder I'm still alone. What man would want to be with a woman who still gets like this over her husband who died so long ago?

"I'm sorry. You probably think I'm a mess. I'm not. Really, I'm not. I think I was just picking up your feelings about your mother and that brought up the past. We can talk about something else so we cheer up, if you want."

I sound desperate. I don't mean to, but I know I do. I just don't want to be alone in this house again for yet another night. Having Cash here makes me feel like at least there's a chance someone in the world might want to spend time with me.

"Did your sister have a good time with her date the other night?" he asks, surprising me that he wants to talk about the wedding again.

"At first I thought you were asking about my older sister but you mean Cheyenne," I answer with a giggle. Cash would have no reason to ask about Cecile after she showed herself to be so rude.

"I think she did. She's so much more fun than I am, so I'm sure he had a much better time than you did too."

Cash quickly says, "If I made you think I didn't have a good time, I'm sorry. I did. Honest. I enjoyed talking to you and the dancing was fun. You didn't step on my toes even once."

"That's sweet of you to say, but I know what I'm like. My sister is wild and free. Even when I was younger than her, I wasn't like that. She's got such a zest for life."

"Some people like that, true. Other people like someone who's like you. My grandmother says there's a pot for every lid. No, it's the opposite way around. A lid for every pot. Yeah, something like that."

I watch as he gets a different look to him when he talks about anything concerning his family. It's like a switch turns on inside him and he brightens up.

"Your family sounds so great, Cash. I like hearing you tell me stories about them. I wish my family was like yours," I admit, genuinely hoping he keeps talking about them.

"You'd fit in perfectly with my family, you know that?" he says with a smile. "They'd love you. No offense, but I think you might have been put with the wrong family. Like someone gave the wrong baby in the nursery at the hospital because other than your younger sister, you're not like any of the others I met."

As much as I hate to admit it, he's right. I don't fit in with anyone but Cheyenne when it comes to my family. They seem intent on being as cruel and callous as possible whenever the chance comes up. My sister and I aren't like that at all, although I'm not sure why considering who we grew up with.

"Cheyenne and I joke that maybe my mother had a long affair with the mailman because she and I are nothing like Cecile, Spencer, or her. We're not even like my father either. The two of us are sort of just over here on an island and they think we're odd."

"I don't think you're odd. I like the way you are. You're kind. I wouldn't be here tonight if you were like your sister Cecile," he says with a laugh before taking a drink of his water.

All that runs through my head is why he actually is here tonight, but I don't ask that question. Maybe he came over because of what happened with his mother and he needed a friend to talk to.

Not that we're exactly friends. A few hours of conversation at a wedding reception can't count as that. I don't know what we are, but at the moment, I'm happy he's here.

Lost in thought about what Cash and I are or what

we're becoming, I hear him say, "I better get going. Tomorrow's an early day."

I work to hide my disappointment, forcing a smile. "Sure. Let me walk you out."

We walk in silence through the house to the front door, and with each step, I silent berate myself for being exactly the kind of person a man can so easily leave. If I was like Cheyenne, he'd stay. That way she has of being so upbeat and fun no matter the situation combined with how strong she always seems makes people want to stick around.

They're drawn to her personality. Mine makes them wish they were somewhere else.

When we reach the door, he turns to face me and I see the distinct signs of a man happy he's about to escape. Relief colors his expression, and in his eyes, there's the surest hint of pity. Whatever I've begun to feel for Cash isn't reciprocated in turn for me.

"Thanks for being so sweet, Savannah. I'm sorry I came over and dumped all my emotional baggage on you. I think this means I owe you."

"Owe me?"

What does he mean by that? Owe me? Is he planning on paying me for our conversation?

"If you want to do something, ask for me like you did this time. I'd like that."

The words enter my brain but get lost so they're swimming in a sea of excitement. Nodding, I smile, loving that he isn't trying to escape and actually liked spending time with me.

And then he leans in and his lips brush against

mine, sending a thrill racing throughout my body. The kiss is soft and tender, but I haven't kissed anyone in two years, so I struggle to keep calm and not act like some twelve year old girl who's never been with someone of the opposite sex.

When I open my eyes, I see him smiling at me. Maybe he liked the kiss too. His blue eyes seem to be sparkling with something I want to think is pleasure.

"I hope we'll see each other again soon, Savannah. Good night."

Barely able to catch my breath, I say, "Good night, Cash."

My heart races while I stand at the door watching him walk to his car. Pressing my lips together, I try to keep the sensation of his mouth on mine alive for as long as possible, loving how incredible that kiss felt.

Our first kiss.

Innocent and sweet, it makes me want more. More kisses. More Cash. More of everything he has to give.

Wait until Cheyenne finds out that I'm not the only one who wants more.

I WANT TO WAIT LONGER, BUT I ONLY MAKE IT TWO days before I call the number again and ask directly for another time with Cash. I know my sister will say I should have pushed it to Friday or Saturday, but Thursday afternoon was as long as I could go.

Something about knowing he wants me to request only him and he wants to see me again too makes this call so much easier than the first or second one. After I finish the call, I wait for hours, expecting to hear about paying like I did the first time. I never heard about payment on Tuesday night, but that doesn't count since we didn't actually go anywhere.

By the time six o'clock rolls around and I haven't heard back about paying, all the things that Cheyenne said the other day begin to echo in my head. When Cash said he wanted me to ask for him when I called again, he didn't mean he wanted to go out on a date like a real couple. He just wanted to make sure he didn't miss out on a job to some other escort.

God, I'm so pathetic. How could I have thought that he felt anything for me?

I sit at my kitchen table waiting for my phone to ring, but as the minutes pass and it gets close to seven, I have to admit the truth. Everything I thought was happening between Cash and me was one-sided. He isn't even interested enough in making money from being with me now.

Heartbroken, I break down and call Cheyenne, needing to speak to someone before I go out of my mind. When she answers and hears the sadness in my voice, she says she'll be right over.

I really am a mess. If I didn't have her, I'd be completely alone, and no one would question why.

Twenty minutes later, Cheyenne breezes into my kitchen with a bottle of red wine and a face that says she's ready to fight. "Tonight, we're getting drunk and if I don't calm down, I'm going to call that service and give them a piece of my mind."

"What's made you so angry?" I ask, unsure I want

to know the answer before I get at least one drink under my belt.

As she pours each of us a glass of wine, she explains, "I'm pissed about that Cash guy. You called and gave him a chance to have a job. That's all this was, and he couldn't even respond? Not cool."

"It's not that important. Just let it go," I say before starting my effort to drown my sorrows.

Cheyenne stands at the kitchen island shaking her head. "No way. I mean, I knew it was never meant to be, but still, even on a business level, this is shitty customer service."

I know she's just being protective of me, but does she have to say things like that? Why couldn't it have worked out with Cash? Is there something inherently wrong with me that makes him wanting to be with me impossible?

Quietly, I try to utter at least a few words to defend myself and why I thought something could happen between us. "He came over on Tuesday night and we talked for almost an hour. It was really nice, Cheyenne, and I thought there was something happening between us."

My sister lets out a sound she only makes when she feels bad for someone. It's a mixture of a huff and a sad groan. Every time I hear it, all I can think is I'm so pathetic, and I'm not the only one who thinks that way.

"Did anything else happen?"

"No. We just talked. Why? What's it matter if

anything else did happen? I'm a grown woman and he's a grown man."

I sound defensive, but I don't care. The way she sounded when she asked if anything else happened made it seem like if it had, Cash would have been taking advantage of me.

"Savannah, it's a question. Nothing else. So all you two did was talk? About what?" she asks as she comes over to the table to continue her interrogation just a few feet from me instead of from across the room.

"His mother was rushed to the hospital, and I think he wanted someone to talk to. Someone who knows what it's like to lose someone they care about. That's it."

My sister twists her face into a scowl before taking a drink of wine. "So he used you because he felt bad and wanted a shoulder to cry on. Nice. Take advantage of a woman who's lost her husband because your mommy had to go to the hospital. Let me guess. She's going to be okay, right?"

I focus on my wine glass and shake it to swirl the red liquid around. "It's not like that, Cheyenne. You don't understand. He was upset. I think he just wanted someone to talk to who understood what he was feeling."

"Uh-huh. You know what I'm hearing? He needed someone to make him feel better, which you did, of course, and then when he was feeling better and heard you requested him, he bailed. I don't know what you did to make him leave that night before making a move, but thank God for it."

What I did? Why is she saying that like I have some natural repellent that chases people away and I activated it just in the nick of time? Maybe I wanted him to make a move.

Even more, I would have loved if he did make a move. I like him. Why is that such a crime to my sister?

"Nothing happened, and not because I did something to turn him off, Cheyenne. He didn't come over here for anything but to talk. Please stop acting like I'm some mindless thing who can't tell if someone's decent or not."

She rolls her eyes at my attempt to stand up for myself. "Well, I'm never using that service again, and I'm going to tell everyone I know who uses them what happened to you. That's not okay. Business is business, and he can't be stopping over at women's houses to look for sympathy and then discard them when he's no longer feeling bad."

"Don't do that. Why are you so sure he acted like that? Maybe they just got busy with so many calls that they haven't gotten back to me yet."

Cheyenne levels her gaze on me, full of judgment for how naïve I sound and her irritation with Cash. "He used you. Just because it wasn't for sex doesn't make it any less wrong. I'm sorry I ever suggested you should use that service, Savannah."

"I think you're wrong. Cash isn't like that. He never did anything that was hurtful or disrespectful, so please stop saying he used me."

My defensiveness inches up notch by notch as I

speak, so that by the time I finish, I'm almost yelling. I never raise my voice with Cheyenne or anyone, for that matter, but sitting here hearing her talk like I'm some idiotic fool and he's just a user makes me angry.

"Okay, okay, but I think you need to just forget him, don't you? I mean, you're already disappointed that you never heard back, even after you gave them all that time today to confirm. I just don't want to see you get hurt from all of this, Savannah. I suggested them, so I'd feel to blame if you did get hurt."

Pouring myself another glass of wine, I force a smile to make her think none of this is really that upsetting to me. "I'm not going to get hurt. I just liked being around him. It was nothing big. Certainly nothing to have you go ruining their business. Don't worry. I'm fine."

She finishes her second glass and shrugs. "Okay, maybe I won't spread the word that they're all bad men no woman should want to be around for any price. I did like Nico, so there's at least one good one. Just promise me you aren't going to blame yourself for anything that happened, okay? Because it's my fault first for getting you involved with these people, and it's that Cash guy's fault for not being very good at his job."

I pretend to find that funny, but the truth is Cash is very good at his job. That's the problem.

CHAPTER FIFTEEN

avannah

AFTER TOO MUCH WINE AND TOO MUCH PRETENDING so my sister wouldn't think I was a hopeless mess pining after Cash, I convinced her I was tired and she finally left by nine o'clock. Ordinarily, I'd love the company for as long as she could stay, but I couldn't listen to how I had mistakenly believed another human being actually liked being around me for another minute.

Grabbing the two wine glasses, I wash them and head toward my room, exhausted from this day. My sister means well, but her effort to be angry on my behalf devolved into a near diatribe on my sad attempt to connect with a man for the first time in two years.

I collapse onto the bed and close my eyes, wishing

that this day would just erase itself from my memory. Whether Cheyenne meant well and Cash didn't, none of it matters. I simply want to forget every minute of this day and wake up tomorrow happy to start a new one with a clean slate.

Maybe I'll get my things and take a trip to the beach. I haven't been there in so long I forget what sand between my toes feels like and what the ocean smells like as you sit in the sun.

As I get lost in making plans for tomorrow, my phone vibrates on my nightstand. Damnit, I thought I turned that off. My sister only wants the best for me, but tonight, she's a bit too much.

My arm over my eyes, I grab the phone with my other hand and blindly swipe across the screen. "Hello."

Usually, I'm a lot friendlier with her, but enough is enough. How many times does she have to lecture me before she thinks I get it? Fine. I'm a fool. It's an escort service, so of course, a man working as an escort wouldn't actually be interested in me.

I'm naïve, not stupid.

When I don't hear anyone talking, I repeat my hello and add, "You really didn't need to call. I'm fine. I was just fantasizing about a day at the beach, so don't worry, I'm fine."

Two fines in one explanation is the international sign that I'm not fine, but hopefully, she doesn't pick up on that. I certainly don't need to spend the next half hour trying to convince her that I am, indeed, fine.

"Savannah, it's Cash. I hope I'm not interrupting anything."

The sound of his deep voice hits me like a slap to my face, and I sit bolt upright in the bed, stunned he's on the phone talking to me. "Cash?"

"Yes. Are you busy?"

Right now, my entire body is shaking. I guess that's technically busy.

I stammer out an answer, still surprised to hear him on my phone. "Uh...n—no, not exactly."

"Well, I was hoping I could come over. I'd like to see you."

Oh, God. Every single word my sister said to me tonight rushes through my brain. He used me to feel better. Of course, he doesn't really have any interest. He works for an escort service. It's his job. Don't be a fool, Savannah.

It was never meant to be.

She's probably right. About all of it. Every last syllable she said to me is probably true. Still, I'm tired of being alone. I'm twenty-seven and should have the right to live my life as I see fit. And if that means making a jackass out of myself because I don't want to be lonely for yet another night, then let me do that. At least it will be fun for a few hours.

So, even though I know I should tell him no, I can't. Loneliness has made me desperate for human interaction. I can't help it.

"Okay. Come over."

Just three simple words, but they feel like a

declaration for me. I'm not going to pretend that living a life of seclusion is what I want. Carson wouldn't want this for me either.

"I'll see you in a little while."

Tossing the phone onto the bed, I look around like I need someone to tell me that just happened. Cash called and wants to see me. Not as a job. To see me as a man sees a woman.

All of this is happening so fast. Should I have said no when he asked to come over? Should I have told him to call me tomorrow? I know exactly what Cheyenne is going to say when she finds out.

"He called because he wanted to get laid. That was a booty call."

Damn, I hope so. Talking is nice, but I'm not in the mood to have a sad conversation about loss tonight.

Nervous but excited, I leap out of bed and hurry over to my closet. What should I wear? Nothing too formal. He's not going to believe I sit around my house in a full length gown. Nothing too casual either, though. I want him to think I look good enough to have sex with, not that I just rolled out of bed.

My eyes scan every outfit on the rod in front of me. My blue capris and that white t-shirt that always looks so nice with it? No. I look too much like a PTA mom in that. I want him to think I look sexy but sweet, not like the mother of a precocious ten year old and the chairwoman of this year's school fundraiser.

What about the red dress with the neckline that plunges halfway down to my belly button? I shake my head. Definitely sexy, but not exactly the vibe I want to give off for our first time together. That dress never felt right on me anyway. Cheyenne convinced me to buy it one time when she dragged me out to a club. I've never worn it again, and I doubt I ever will.

I lift the hanger holding that pink dress Carson always said I looked so beautiful in every time I wore it. I've loved this dress from the moment I saw it in the store. The shade of pink is light but looks great against my skin.

No, I shouldn't wear that. It wouldn't be right.

As I set that back on the rod, I spy the white sundress I bought a while back. It's perfect! Not too formal but not too casual either. It shows off just enough to make me look sexy while letting me feel comfortable with my sweet side.

Grabbing it, I rush back across the room and toss it onto the bed before I begin to get undressed. I need to check my hair and my makeup after I put the dress on. I want everything to be as perfect as possible.

It isn't every day a woman gets to end her dry spell of a couple years.

THE DOORBELL RINGS, AND MY HEART NEARLY bursts out of my chest. This is going to be fine, Savannah. Just relax. You're two people getting together to have a good time. Nothing more. Don't put pressure on yourself to be anything but who you are.

A woman who wants to have sex with a good looking man.

I check out my reflection in the mirror in the hallway near the front door and take a deep breath in. My makeup and hair look good. My favorite white sundress is doing its job to make my tan look even better than it actually is.

Damn, I should have put on some perfume. Too late now.

As I open the door, I take another deep breath in and try to relax. This is what happens when you don't date for two years. A simple visit from someone you like makes you react like it's some major state event.

Cash stands on the doorstep looking as good as always. Dressed in a black t-shirt and a pair of jeans that hang low on his hips, he smiles like he's happy to see me.

"Come in. I was surprised you called tonight. I didn't think I'd hear from you."

He walks in with all the confidence I wish I possessed right now. No matter. Yes, it's been a while since I was with someone, but it's like riding a bike. You never forget how to do it.

When I close the door, he says in a low voice, "I got your message that you wanted to get together."

Confused, I turn around and shake my head. "I never got any call about paying. I waited, but I never heard back, so..."

I don't want to finish that sentence. That's not what I want tonight to be. Not that I necessarily have a problem with paying him for sex, to be honest. That's no different than paying him to escort me to my brother's wedding reception. I just hoped that tonight wouldn't be about business.

Cash steps toward me and shakes his head. "I'm not here on a job, Savannah. I'm here because I like you."

I want to say I like him too, but all that comes out of my mouth is a single, almost squeaky word. "Oh."

He's so close now, mere inches away, and he sounds different than any other time I've heard his voice. It's deeper but softer, like he's trying not to scare me off.

His finger trails down my forearm as he takes another step toward me, shrinking the space between us to practically nothing. "And I think you like me."

My breath catches in my chest when I open my mouth to admit the truth that I do like him. More than like. I want him to help me banish the loneliness that's been my constant companion in this house for the past two years.

At least for tonight.

"I do. I do like you, Cash."

With a smile that makes me feel like I'm melting, he says, "Good." A second later, he dips his head and his lips brush against the skin just below my neck, sending ripples of desire over every inch of my body.

My eyelids flutter closed, and at the first touch of his tongue to my neck, I move my hands up to run my fingers through his hair. I've waited to touch it from the moment he appeared at my door that day to take me to the wedding. Jet black and thick, I imagined it would feel incredible, but now as I let it glide over my skin, I'm surprised to find it so soft.

His hands find my waist and then move up to cup my breasts, pushing me back against the front door as he begins his exploration of my body. His touch is gentle but insistent, and I welcome it and anything else he has to offer.

My mind fills with how good this feels to have someone want me again. I inhale a deep breath, taking the earthy scent of his cologne into me. He smells warm and inviting, like a sensual summer night out in the woods under the stars with all of nature around you.

Tilting his hips, he presses his body against my belly and I know he's aroused. He feels long and thick, and my desire ratchets up a notch at what awaits me.

"Do you want to move this to somewhere more comfortable?" he whispers in a husky voice next to my ear.

I don't know the answer to that question. All I know is I don't want the way he makes me feel to stop.

Cash leans back to look into my eyes and smiles. "I'm fine with right here, but I'm sure you know where's more comfortable in your own house."

Without thinking, I take his hand and begin to walk toward my bedroom. I don't know where this bravery is coming from. I've never been this assertive in my life, but I want tonight to be something I can remember forever.

He wraps his arms around my waist and nuzzles my neck as we climb the stairs to the second floor. I slide my hands over his as they rest against my abdomen and think about how I can't wait for what's about to happen.

His skin is warm, and I run my palms up his forearms, teasing the hair with my fingertips. It feels masculine, and when he groans against my neck as we reach the top of the stairs, my body reacts to that sound that tells me he wants this as much as I do.

"Which room is yours?" he asks, tearing me out of the momentary ecstasy I'm enjoying at these simple preludes to what's about to happen.

I point down the hall and turn my head to look at him. "The third room. We can go anywhere, though."

Why I say that out loud I have no idea. I've wondered how I'd deal with the first time I slept with another man in this house. I moved out of our bedroom a week after the funeral, unable to sleep alone in the bed Carson and I shared. Too many memories and ghosts haunted me in that room, and even though I wasn't ready then to move on, I knew if I stayed there night after night, I'd become trapped in the past. As much as I wanted to remain there, I couldn't.

Cash stops us in front of the first room, and I freeze. It shouldn't matter. Two years have passed. My husband doesn't live here anymore. He doesn't live anywhere, except in my memories. He'd want me to keep living. I know him. He'd wonder what the hell took me so long and would probably chastise me for living like I have for all this time.

"Third room, okay. It's your choice, Savannah."

I turn in his hold to look at him to see if he knows what's running through my mind. He's so beautiful standing here in front of me, his blue eyes boring into me full of desire.

"Cash..."

Whatever I wanted to say a moment ago evaporates into the haze of need that takes me over when he leans down to kiss me. His soft lips tease mine for a long moment before he flicks his tongue into my mouth and stuffs his hand into my hair to gently tug my head back. An ache forms between my legs, growing with every second we kiss and take another step toward my room.

I've always been submissive when it comes to being with men. It's nothing I've ever chosen to be. It's just who I am. With Cash, though, I have more courage than ever before, although I'm not sure why because part of me fears what's coming as much as the rest of me wants it so badly.

Sliding my hands down his chest, I tug his t-shirt out of his jeans and touch his stomach. A thin dusting of hair covers his torso, and taut muscles strain beneath his skin. He's hardness under softness, heat behind a cool exterior, gentleness alongside power.

And I want it all.

He guides me into my bedroom, all the while keeping our mouths locked in a kiss. I pull his shirt up toward his shoulders to take it off, and he pulls away for only the second it takes to lift the shirt over his head and toss it onto the floor. I glance at his half naked body and press my lips together, partly missing the feel of his mouth on mine and partly to stop the moan that threatens to escape as I admire how gorgeous he is.

I lean toward him to kiss him again, but his focus is on stripping my dress off. Sliding his hands up under the skirt, he glides his palms over the front of my thighs, up over my hips and breasts, until he's ready to lift it over my head.

"Arms up," he says, practically on a moan.

I do as he tells me to, and a second later, I'm standing in front of him in my white bra and panties. Reaching out to touch him, I miss him as he backs up, his gaze rolling over my body and making me feel exposed.

But then, he levels his gaze on my face and licks his lips. "I love that you're in white."

As I kick off my shoes and push them under the bed, I ask, "Why?"

"Because it fits. You seem innocent. Are you innocent, Savannah?"

The truth is I probably am, simply because I haven't been with a man for so long, but I don't want to be that. I want to be seductive and sensual, a temptress he can't say no to. A goddess he seeks to please. Innocence implies he needs to be careful with me. I don't want that.

I want him to be hard and forceful, to give me what I've craved night after night.

So I shake my head to answer his question.

Taking a step toward me, he runs his fingertips along my collarbone before dipping his head to place a soft kiss in the hollow at the base of my neck. It sends chills down my spine, and I shiver.

Cash looks up into my eyes and gives me a wicked smile. "I think you are innocent, but you won't be after tonight."

I have no idea what that means, but I can't wait to find out.

CHAPTER SIXTEEN

ash

Jesus, this woman has an effect on me. Standing there in just her white lace bra and panties, she looks like every guy's innocent virgin fantasy come to life. Add to that her staring up at me with those big brown eyes like she isn't sure what I'm about to do to her, and I don't think my cock could get any harder.

I waited for hours before finally giving in to my desire to be with her. I've never slept with a client. Hell, I haven't been on a job with one before Savannah in so long I can't remember who the last one was.

Damon and I always had an unwritten rule when we were actually doing the escort jobs. No sleeping with the clients. Not even the incredibly gorgeous ones who practically begged to be fucked. Nope.

I prided myself on the fact that I never did back then, even though a few times I was tempted, and then when we hired enough guys to take the jobs so we could simply be the managers of the business, that problem became a non-issue. Since then, I've enjoyed life as the magician behind the curtain setting up our employees with the lovely women who need their services.

Until Savannah.

Maybe I shouldn't have come over here the other night after dealing with what happened to my mother, but since then, I haven't been able to think of anything but seeing Savannah again and finding out what this could become. I have a feeling she thinks this is all in the line of duty, that the other night and tonight are merely me doing my job as an escort, but that's not it.

I'm here because for the first time in a long time, I can't get a woman off my mind. I know myself well enough. Once she became all I could think about, I knew this would end up happening. It was just a matter of when, not if.

Savannah's hand brushes against my chest, and she sets it right above my heart. "You got quiet there. Is everything okay?"

I run my fingertips over her shoulders and push the satin bra straps down onto her arms. She lets out a tiny moan that goes straight through me. I know she's not really innocent, but there's something about her that makes me think she hasn't been with a man in the two years since her husband died.

That's a long time to be alone without anyone touching you for a twenty-seven year old woman.

She reaches out and slides her finger along the top of my jeans, teasing the skin between my hips. "Did you flinch when I touched you?" she asks with a smile.

"Maybe a little," I answer honestly.

"I want to think you're as nervous as I am, but that's not true, is it? You probably think I'm silly for being like I am," she says shyly, lowering her head so I can't see her eyes.

Lifting her chin with my finger, I see she's afraid. "Not silly at all. You seem innocent."

"Do you like that?"

"I like that with you."

After a few seconds, she exhales, and I realize she's been holding her breath since she confessed she was nervous. "You know, I'm not that innocent. I just look it now because I've been alone in this house too long. Please don't feel like you need to treat me like I'm some doll who might break. I'm like any other woman. Honest."

Her frankness makes me like her even more, and I smile at how sweet she is. "Trust me. You're not like any other woman."

Her fingers nimbly take care of the button on my pants, and she smiles up at me with a seductive look in her eyes that says she wants to show me just how little innocence she has. She lowers my zipper slowly, inch by inch, making me wait for her touch on me. It's like torture, but I like seeing her like this.

"I had a fantasy the other night that I'd like to live

out. Do you mind?" she asks before sitting on the bed in front of me.

Shaking my head, I see her open my pants and palm my cock. Her touch is gentle and warm, and she gives me one last look before closing her eyes and leaning down to wrap her lips around me.

Do I mind a woman going down on me? Not at all. Savannah runs her tongue along the bottom of my shaft, teasing my balls when she reaches the base and takes every inch of me into her mouth. My innocent knows how to suck cock.

I watch in rapt amazement as she works me in and out between her lips, up and down from head to base, all the while her arms wrapped around my legs so her hands cup my ass. I touch her head, stuffing my hand into her hair to set the pace so I don't come too quickly, and she looks up at me with the sexiest expression in her eyes as my cock pops out of her mouth.

"Pull my hair. I love that when I'm going down on a man," she says in a husky voice completely unlike how she usually sounds.

Her wish is my command, especially if it adds to her pleasure which can only add to my own. I twist my fingers in her hair at the back of her head, the dark strands tightening against my skin as she lowers to take my cock into her mouth again.

When she reaches the base, she presses her fingertips into my ass and pulls me to her. Her tongue swipes my balls, sending my need to come into overdrive. Giving her hair a hard tug, I pull her up so only the tip remains between her lips. It's the sexiest fucking thing I've ever seen when she flicks her tongue around it and smiles up at me.

"That's it, baby. Make me come."

Her eyes open wide, like that excites her, and she pulls my body to her again, swallowing every inch of my cock in a rush. Now I don't want to slow her down so I have to wait for my release. I want to fill that pretty mouth and watch her swallow everything I give her.

She sucks hard and fast, like I've never had anyone go down on me before. It's anything but sweet, but she still has an innocence to her even now that I can't get enough of. I pull her hair harder each time she bobs down onto me, so hard that I know she must be in pain.

But I never hear anything like a cry or a plea for me to stop. All I hear are the sound of her beautiful mouth and tongue against my skin and tiny moans as I get closer to coming.

On the last time down my shaft, she hums against the base, and that's all it takes. The first jet of cum shoots out of me, and she takes every last drop. Tilting her head back, I watch her swallow each time I fill her mouth, her gaze pinning me to the spot.

I thrust my hips so the head of my cock pushes up against the back of her throat one last time, and she swallows hard, her throat contracting around me. It's like nothing I've ever felt in my life.

Raw, erotic, powerful. Savannah.

When there's nothing more inside me, she falls

back on the bed and smiles. Her hair lays around her head, fanned out like she's a goddess staring up at me.

Pressing her lips together, she moans softly. "That was even better than what I fantasized. Thank you."

"I'm glad I'm the lucky guy who got to live it out with you."

Savannah licks her lips and reaches out to pull me down on top of her. "You should be since you were the one in my fantasy, after all."

While I slide her panties off her legs and fumble around behind her to get that bra off, I ask, "When did you have that? After the wedding or after the other night?"

She opens her legs and wraps them around my thighs. "The other night. After you kissed me."

"I should get these pants off," I say, just realizing she's naked beneath me and I'm still half-dressed.

Lifting herself off the bed, she kisses me long and deep, and I taste myself on her tongue when she slides it over mine. "Allow me."

Behind me, her feet push my pants and boxer briefs down my legs until they're almost hanging off my ankles. I look down to see her focused on getting them those last few inches, like it's a task she's ready to put her heart and soul into.

She bites her lower lip, intent on finishing the job, but then frowns after a few tries. "I think you're going to have to kick them off. They're fighting me."

As I wriggle them off my feet, happy to finally be free to move the way I want to with her, she cradles my face and looks up at me so sweetly that if I hadn't just watched her suck my cock like a woman who knows what she's doing, I'd think she was that virginal creature I'd fantasized about last night. It's confusing and exciting all at the same time, like the perfect woman, my own personal madonna and whore all in one.

"I've been wet since I went down on you, so please don't make me wait any more, Cash," she says, almost whining that she wants me to fuck her.

I tilt my hips to press my cock against her pussy, and I feel how ready she is for me. "I thought I might return the favor and go down on you first."

She shakes her head and pouts. "No. We can do that another time. Right now, I just want to feel you inside me."

Excitement courses through every inch of my body. Lifting my hips, I angle my cock between her open legs and that beautiful cunt I plan on feasting on later. She's ready and waiting, and with one slow push into her, I'm balls deep inside her pussy.

Fuck, she's wet! And hot, like her body is ready to overheat. A loud moan fills my ears, and looking down at her, I see her biting her lip. Is she in pain? She said she hasn't been with a man in a long time.

"Does that feel okay?" I ask, suddenly afraid I'm hurting her.

Savannah smiles and runs her fingernails down my chest. Pulling her legs back toward the bed, she opens herself up as much as she can.

"It feels incredible. God, fuck me. Fast. I want to feel you fill me up."

Her heels press hard into the base of my spine, urging me to give her all she wants. I kiss her like her lips are all I need to survive and begin pumping into her, fucking like I'm a man on a mission.

I am.

I want to possess her. I want to claim her so no man can be here like this with her but me. I want her innocence to be all mine, and when she wants to be satisfied, I want to be the man she calls.

Not some other guy I hired to give women like her a good time. Not some guy she meets at some party who doesn't care that she's tender and kind and only wants to fuck her.

I want to be the only one she thinks of when she wants a man.

She whimpers as I feel her getting close, but still she drags her fingernails over the skin near my shoulder blades and begs for more. "Oh, God... harder...please..."

My cock pistons into her wet cunt, my desperate goal the same as hers. I want to feel that release she's dying for, buried inside her until there's nothing but the two of us joined together.

The first twinge of her orgasm makes her body tighten around my cock, and she sinks her teeth into my shoulder, sending waves of pain to mix with the pleasure racing through me. I notice it but can't stop, even if I wanted to.

When her cunt contracts and she cries out, begging me not to stop, I know she's at that spot I'll reach in just a few seconds more. I don't stop pumping into her, my hips sore from how hard I'm fucking her, and then she moans into my ear as waves of release wash over her.

Mine happens a minute or so later, and I thrust into her body one last time before I come. I lay still on top of her, the only movement the twitch of my cock as I fill her up. It's perfect, better than anything I've ever felt before in my life.

Savannah looks up at me, searching my expression for something, and I smile before collapsing onto the bed next to her. Fuck, that was intense.

"Cash, that was great. Thank you."

I turn to look at her and can't believe how beautiful she looks right now. "No need to thank me. I've never had sex be anything like that, so I'm thinking it was all you."

Her cheeks turn pink from a blush. Burying her head in my shoulder, she says quietly, "I think I might have sounded like some wild woman back there. I've never been like that before with any man."

She's so sweet, and I lean over to press a kiss to the top of her head. "Well, I liked it."

After a few seconds, she looks up at me with hesitation in her eyes. "I guess you do that a lot in your job."

For the first time, I want to tell her the whole truth about me and who I am. I'm so fucking tired of lying to everyone in my life, and it would be nothing to share who I really am with Savannah.

But I can't bring myself to go all the way, so I share the truth I can with her.

"Actually, no. I've never slept with anyone I worked with."

She lifts herself up onto her elbow and shakes her head, like she can't believe that. "Really? I just thought that you didn't like me enough to do it after the wedding. Then I wondered if you just wanted to be friends after the other night." She stops and lowers her gaze to avoid facing me. "So nobody else before me?"

"Yep. Nobody. I guess I'm just not the kind of escort women want to sleep with."

That makes her lift her eyes, and in them, I see disbelief. "No way. I don't know what those other women were thinking, but you're definitely the type of man women want."

"Then that works because you're definitely the type of woman this man wants."

CHAPTER SEVENTEEN

*S*avannah

THE MOMENT I OPEN MY EYES, I KNOW SOMETHING'S different. I'm barely awake, but it's instantly a feeling like the world's changed.

Because it has.

At my side, Cash sleeps with his arms around me and his face nuzzled up against my neck. I turn to watch him, sure I've never seen anyone so peaceful in my entire life. He looks like a little boy curled up next to me, quietly breathing in and out so his chest rises and falls.

Except he's not a boy. He's a grown man who rocked my world last night, and if I'm not careful, a man who's going to make being with any other man again an impossibility.

I've only felt this way once before in my life. I

remember being unsure about that then too. He was too old for me. I was supposed to fall for someone my age. Nobody thought we were right for each other.

The way I met Cash isn't the way a relationship is supposed to start either. I'm supposed to meet someone my family thinks will give me a safe and secure life. Or to many people, I'm supposed to live out the rest of my life in this house, only going out when it seems appropriate but never actually living.

I didn't let the uncertainty of what we could be keep me from falling for Carson, and I'm not going to let it get in the way of whatever Cash and I can have. I've spent too many nights alone dreaming of what my life could be to let that happen.

As I watch, he lifts his head and opens his eyes. His vision bleary, he stares up at me for a long moment, and I can't help but think he's got the bluest eyes I've ever seen.

"Morning."

It takes a few seconds for him to respond, but after he scrubs the last bit of sleep from his face, he turns over toward me and smiles. "Have you been awake for long?"

"No. Just a little while. I didn't want to move and disturb you since you were sound asleep."

Stretching his arms, he makes a groaning sound that's purely masculine. "I must have been tired. Or maybe it's that this bed is like heaven. I'm not sure I want to ever get up."

"Do you have to go already?" I ask, hoping I don't sound too clingy.

He shakes his head and leans over to kiss me softly on the cheek. "No, and between you and this bed, I'm going to have a hard time convincing myself to go when it's time."

Before I can say another word, he pulls me into his arms and I close my eyes, loving how he feels next to me. He's muscular and strong, and I'm convinced I'm safer with him than I've ever been in my life.

"What are you doing today?" I ask, curious to know more about his everyday life.

He sighs against me and answers, "I was thinking I'd drive back down to Tampa to see my mother, but I don't think I want to stay the night. Do you have something planned?"

I never have anything planned. That sounds sad, but it's the truth. I wake up every day and wander around this house until someone calls me or it's time to go to bed again.

"No. I was just wondering what you do with your days. Just curious."

That sounds defensive. I don't mean it to. I just don't want Cash to think I'm prying.

When he doesn't say anything, I add, "I mean, I know you have your restaurant to manage, so I don't expect you to lay around here all day with me."

I wait for him to mention the name of his restaurant, but I don't want to push. When he wants to tell me, he will.

Cash sighs again and then he leans back away and smiles. "Everyone gets a day off, so I might want to lay around here with you all day. I can't think of anything else I'd rather do."

Suddenly, an idea comes to me from out of the blue. It's crazy and he'll probably think I'm being too clingy, but I don't stop myself from suggesting it.

"Would you like to go to the beach sometime?"

He narrows his eyes for a moment and then shrugs. "I haven't been to the beach in years, you know that? Ever since I moved away and came up here. I guess I'm always too busy and never think of it anymore."

I instantly feel like I've pushed too hard too fast with him. "It's okay. I can go anytime, so it's no big deal. It just popped into my head, so I thought I'd mention it."

Now my defensiveness rages out of control, and if I don't get out of this bed soon, I'm going to end up saying something ridiculous and chasing him away forever. I gently push off his chest and roll over to get up.

More like escape before I ruin everything.

His arms catch me and pull me back to the warmth of his body, though, and he nuzzles his chin with its new hair growth against my shoulder. He's passionate and sexy, and I want to think I didn't mess things up.

"Where are you going? No fair mentioning going to the beach and then rushing off like that. Unless you changed your mind."

I quickly turn in his hold so we're face to face. "I didn't change my mind at all. I just thought that maybe you felt like I was rushing things too much."

Embarrassed, I lower my head so I don't have to face him. I stare down at his chest and remember how his skin smelled like his cologne last night.

"You aren't rushing anything, Savannah. I'd love to go to the beach with you. What about tomorrow?"

I look up and see him waiting for my answer like he's truly worried I might say I don't want to or that tomorrow isn't good enough. "That would be great! We can make a day of it, if that's okay with your schedule."

"Tell you what. I'll make it okay. You pick the beach, and we'll go and do whatever you want."

Overwhelmed by how happy I am, I hug him tightly, loving how he feels against me. "Thank you, Cash!"

I feel him hard against me, and inch back away from him. "Sorry for squishing you like that. I was just excited about us going to the beach."

He chuckles and lifts the covers to look beneath them. "And I'm excited for an entirely different reason."

For a second or two, I'm not sure what to say. I've never been a fan of morning sex, no matter how many times I hear how great it is. I'm weird like that. My mouth usually tastes like I've eaten a pound of cotton fibers when I wake up, and the thought of kissing someone seems gross.

"Well, I'm going to go grab some coffee. I'll be right back."

He doesn't get a chance to pull me back this time, and I jump out of bed to grab my t-shirt off the chair near the window and panties off the floor before hurrying down to the kitchen. Maybe I have something minty somewhere in the cabinets I can quickly eat before I go back upstairs. At least then if he wants to have sex again, I won't be worried I taste like I spent the night eating my pillowcase.

I search my kitchen but only find an old pack of spearmint gum that's probably five years old. When I stick it in my mouth, it crumbles into half a dozen pieces, none of which contains much flavor.

So much for fresh breath.

Spitting the gum out into my hand, I toss it into the garbage and hurry back upstairs to find Cash out of bed and in the shower already. He probably thought he should get ready and leave as quickly as possible after my odd bolting downstairs.

I push open the bathroom door and see him standing behind the glass doors as steam rises around him. God, he's beautiful. A gorgeous body, a face like chiseled marble, and a cock that made me orgasm three times last night.

And what am I? The woman who thinks she should leave the bed she's in with him to find a piece of old, dusty gum.

"What happened to the coffee?" he asks from inside the shower.

I take a step closer and see his hair is pushed off his face, and he looks more stunning than ever. I could be in there with him, if I wasn't such an awkward mess. If I hadn't bolted from the bed like I was on fire.

"What?" I ask, suddenly realizing he asked me a question.

He smiles and shakes his head. "The coffee? You said you were going to make some."

The coffee! Oh my God! I never made any. I got so fixated on finding something that would make my morning breath go away that it completely slipped my mind.

"Oh, yeah. The coffee maker didn't want to work. I guess I need a new one," I say, wishing I had a better lie.

Talk about not being able to think on my feet. All I can think of at the moment, though, is how incredible Cash looks wet.

The shower door opens out toward me, and he crooks his finger to beckon me in. "Then there's no reason you shouldn't join me. Get in here so we can enjoy this together."

I'm sure he means the six shower heads that make you feel like you're getting a massage as you wash your hair, but I don't say a word and simply strip out of my t-shirt and panties. As I step inside, he pulls me close and kisses me deeply, and all I can taste is mint on his tongue.

Sliding his hands down my body, he cups my ass and smiles. "I hope you don't mind. I took a little of your toothpaste. I'm all about sex in the morning, but I have a thing with morning breath. It's a little OCD, but it's how I am."

As I gaze up into his beautiful face, I smile at his confession. "Me too. I hope I taste okay."

The water rolls down over his forehead, hitting his straight nose and falling into his mouth when he smiles and says, "Let's see."

And then he kisses me again, and I feel like I'm soaring, even as the hot water from the shower drenches me. His hands pull me into his body, and his hard on presses against my pussy. I want to feel him inside me again. I should be sore after all the sex we had last night, but my body craves more of him.

When he pulls away, he says, "You taste great up here. Now to see about the other place I want to taste."

As much as I would love that, I shake my head when he begins to crouch down in front of me. Confused, he looks up at me like he doesn't understand.

"Not a fan of oral? If you give me a chance, I think I can change your mind."

His thumbs open me up to him, but it's not that I don't like having someone go down on me. "It's not that. I just would prefer to have you inside me."

A smile that grows broader by the second lifts the corners of his mouth, and he stands up to his full height to kiss me. "Hard to say no to that, but I do want to lick that pretty pussy of yours sometime soon."

Before I can say a word, he lifts me into the air and lowers me down onto his hard cock. God, it feels so good as each inch fills me, stretching my body to take all he is.

"When I get sick of this, you can do that," I say when I get all of him inside me.

He holds me to him, making sure I don't fall while I cling to his neck and ride his cock. "Then we have a problem because I'm not willing to give this up."

I kiss him, loving how good he tastes and how full he makes me feel with every time he slides into me. "Me neither."

Along with the steam, the sounds of our lovemaking fill the shower, his grunts every time he fills me up and my moans to let him know how much I love how he makes me feel. Our mouths seek out one another, our lips sliding sloppily against our slick skin. His beard scrapes me, but I love the sensation and how masculine he looks without a shave.

I sense my orgasm growing inside me and say in his ear, "I'm so close. God, I want to come. Don't stop."

His hand pulls at my hair, sending tiny shots of pain across the top of my head, as he moans, "Come for me, baby. I want to feel your cunt tighten around me and make me come."

The sound of his voice, strained and low like he's barely holding on, sends me over the edge, and a second later, I cry out. My fingernails scrape across his back, and I buck my hips with wild abandon, milking his cock with everything my body has.

Cash pushes me down onto him hard, his hands on my waist forcing my body to give him what he needs until he stills and wraps his arms around me. I feel him come, filling me with all he has, and I close my eyes to take it all with the hot water running down my face.

Exhausted, I cling to his neck when he lowers me onto the tile floor and smiles down at me. I know I shouldn't think that I'm falling for him right after great sex. It's just a physical reaction. Nothing more.

Yet, when I look up at him, I can't help myself. I am falling for Cash, and I don't want to stop myself. For the first time in two years, I want to enjoy something and not feel guilty.

ash

MY MOTHER LAUGHS AT MY COMMENT ABOUT making the trip back to Tampa in less than seventy minutes. She thinks I'm joking. It's probably not a good idea to tell her the truth and upset her.

"Honey, I'm fine. You can come here if your schedule allows it, but you don't have to worry. I feel great now."

"Are you sure?"

"I promise, Cash. You don't have to be worried. I want you to focus on your schoolwork, okay?"

Her first mention of my supposedly still attending law school makes my stomach twist into a knot. I have to tell her. I should tell her right now. Today is as good a day as any other day, and she did say she feels great.

Then again, she did just spend a weekend in the

hospital after falling unconscious not a week ago. Maybe I should wait a little while longer.

All the better since I still haven't figured out what the hell I'm going to say when I finally do tell her the truth. Just thinking about it makes me cringe. She's going to get that look in her eyes. I know it.

"You're not keeping your head in the books all the time, are you, honey? I know you spent some time with your brother when you were here last, but you do get out sometimes when you're at school, right?"

I open my mouth to tell her about the day I spent with Savannah and how we're planning on going to the beach tomorrow, but I stop myself. That would only open up the possibility that she'd ask more about what I've been doing lately, and that would mean more lies.

Fuck, I'm so tired of lying. Lying about law school. Lying about the successful business I have. Lying about meeting someone as incredible as Savannah.

So many lies. I can't wait until the truth all comes out. No matter how disappointed everyone will be, at least this burden will be off my shoulders and I can breathe a sigh of relief finally.

"Yes, Mom. I get out so I don't grow roots to the furniture."

The smile in her voice comes through loud and clear. "Okay, honey. Go have a wonderful night, and please don't worry about me. I promise I'm fine."

"I'll talk to you in a couple days. Tell Dad if anything happens, I want him to call me immediately."

She sighs, like she hates that we're all watching her

so carefully. "I will. Love you, Cash."

"I love you too, Mom. Talk to you soon."

Hearing her sound so upbeat and happy makes me think I don't need to drive back there today. That will give me some time tonight to catch up on setting up jobs for the guys before going with Savannah to the beach tomorrow.

I sit down on the sofa and start listening to clients' messages and plotting out which guy would work for which job. Fifteen minutes into work, a knock at my door gives me a reason to take a break and stretch my legs.

Damon said he'd be stopping over tonight or tomorrow, so if it's him, that's great. This way, I won't have to come back early from the beach with Savannah to handle work with him.

Lost in thought about a job I think Nico would be good for, I open the door to see not Damon but Emily, my ex-girlfriend who I told never to come here again. Dressed in a tiny skirt and tank top, she looks like she has plans for this visit I want no part of.

"Go home, Em."

Instantly, her ruby red lower lip juts out into a pout that never fails to work on anyone. It used to work on me. It doesn't anymore.

"Cash, come on. Let me in. I just want to talk to you. If you'd answer my texts, I wouldn't have to come here and bother you," she says in that baby voice of hers she thinks is sexy.

"If I answered your texts, you'd still come over. You know that and I know that, so stop the bullshit."

My unwillingness to play her little game frustrates her, so she skips more baby talk and jumps to the next level. Seduction. Emily has few tricks, and I know them all, so this doesn't surprise me.

Pressing her hand to my stomach, she traces tiny circles against my shirt with her forefinger. "Come on. Why can't you be nice? I think I deserve it."

"Deserve what?" I ask, instantly hating myself for giving her another chance to start a conversation.

I know better than this with her. Why did I take the bait? She'll use any in she can to continue whatever this is we're doing.

She surprises me by stepping forward and kissing me. When I move away to stop her, she sneaks under my arm, hurrying into my apartment. Fuck. That's the last thing I need now.

Turning on my heel, I spin around to see her starting to make herself at home in my living room. If she plants herself on my sofa, I'm not above physically removing her and carrying her out to get her to leave.

I catch up with her and grab her arm to stop her before she gets comfortable. She looks up at me and gives me one of her hurt faces.

"Cash, why are you being like this? I know you miss me as much as I miss you."

What I definitely don't miss is that fucking whining tone to her voice. That I could never hear again and be perfectly happy for all time.

"We're over, Em. That's why I never answer your texts. There's nothing to say."

She slides her hand down my chest and smiles.

"That's not true and you know it. Did you see my bikini pic I posted the other day? I got so many likes for that pic, and everyone said I looked incredible. What did you think?"

I grab her wrists to stop her from touching me since I know where she'll be going for next. "I didn't see it. I've been busy."

Emily frowns and turns to look at my notes on the coffee table. "You're still doing that thing with Damon? I would have thought that would have ended by now since you left school nearly two years ago."

I cringe at her making any comment on our business. I wish I never told her a thing about it. That's what I get for thinking I was in love.

"Baby, please let go of my arms. I want to show you the pic."

As I tug her toward the door, I shake my head. "That's okay. I can use my imagination. You need to go, though."

"Why? You're just sitting here all alone."

Tired of being nice, I snap, "Because I'm leaving to go to my parents' house. My mother's sick, so I need to go see her."

For a split second, I think I see concern in her eyes, but that disappears when she gets her hands from my hold and palms my cock. "Come on, Cash. I know what makes you happy. Let me do what you love and take the stress away before you go."

I push her away, but that doesn't faze her. Instead, she drops to her knees and starts to unzip my pants. What the fuck is wrong with this woman?

Disgusted, I shove her so she falls to the floor. "I just told you my mother's sick and I'm going home to see her, and all you can think about is sucking my cock? What the fuck is missing in you that you think that's okay?"

Her hands claw at my thighs, her fingernails trailing up toward my zipper. "I love you, Cash. You love me too. I know you do. We belong together."

Fuck, I hate this shit she pulls. Normally, I can ignore Emily's desperate attempts to get me back, but now when I look down at her begging to blow me, all I want to do is find a way to forget her forever.

"No, we don't."

"Do you remember telling me you thought we'd get married? I'd make you a perfect wife. Look at me, Cash. I'm what a man like you marries. I don't care that you aren't going to be a lawyer. I don't even care if you want to keep doing that thing with Damon."

I hate everything about her now. How could I have thought I loved this person? Everything about her sickens me. The long nails she obsesses about, like they fucking mean anything to anyone but her. Her fake tits she loves to whip out whenever anyone shows her the tiniest bit of attention. The expensive purse that's one of dozens she owns all because of the name on it.

What did I care about when I was with her?

Lifting her up by the waist, I set her on her feet and start moving her toward the door. "It's over, Em. I'm seeing someone else now, so don't do this anymore. It's embarrassing, and it isn't going to work."

Shock fills her expression, and all she can do is shake her head. "What do you mean seeing someone? You never go out, Cash. You spend all your time working on that stupid business with Damon."

I push her a few feet more toward the door before she stops dead. "Did you meet someone doing that? You told me you never honestly felt anything for those women. Is that where you met her? Because you never go anywhere, so if you met someone, that's the only place you'd find her."

That's it. I'm done playing games with her.

Grabbing her arm, I squeeze my fingers into her flesh and tug her to get her to leave. "Fuck off, Em. I tried being nice to you. You don't know how to take a hint. We're done. I'm finished with you and your endless pit of need. Go find someone else to fill that for you because I'm out. Don't come back because I have nothing more for you."

Tears fill her eyes, and she shakes her head. "I don't believe that. We aren't finished. Not by a long shot. I'm not going to lose you to some pathetic thing who has to hire someone to take her out. No fucking way, Cash. We're meant to be. You know it."

I open the door and shove her out into the hallway. She barely stays on her feet, and when she turns around to face me, I see clearly why I could never care for Emily the way I want to care for a woman. She's merely a vain bitch who collects things, and I was one of those things.

That's not the kind of woman I want. Not anymore.

CHAPTER NINETEEN

avannah

CASH TOSSES THE END OF THE RED AND BLUE striped towel away from him and attempts to lay it down on the sand. He only half succeeds, and it ends up looking like he merely threw it onto the ground with much less effort than he actually made.

Frustrated, he frowns and turns to look at me. "They always make it look so easy in the movies. This beach is killing my cool guy vibe I'm trying to project."

I don't want to laugh at him because he seems so discouraged and he's clearly trying so hard to be this cool guy he thinks I want. Stifling my chuckle, I nod like I understand the seriousness of all of this and step over the crumpled up beach towel so I'm standing on the other side of it opposite him.

"Why don't we try it with me holding this end and

you grabbing the other end? Then we can just lay it down and everything will be good."

He nods, but I get the sense he was really hoping to amaze me with some fantastic towel spreading out maneuver. "That could work."

Crouching down, I take hold of my side of the beach towel and look up to see him take his side. When I set mine down, he follows and smiles like we've achieved something today.

"Let's hope things improve from here. Not being able to master the beach towel doesn't bode well for our day at the beach."

I smile at his attempt at being cute, but I get the feeling he's nervous. What I don't understand is why. It's not like we barely know one another. We've already slept together, so why would he be uneasy around me?

Then the truth hits me out of the blue. He's embarrassed to be with me in public. But why? I look like any other woman here on this beach. In fact, I'd say I look at least as good as the rest of these women. I'm a little pale, but that happens when you don't go out much. Maybe I should have used some self-tanner so I wouldn't look like a ghost out here today.

"Savannah, Earth to Savannah. Did you hear me?"

I shake my head to rid my mind of the questions racing through my brain. "No. What?"

Cash smiles sweetly at me. "You looked like you were a million miles away there. I asked you if you wanted me to go get anything from the stand. I was thinking I'd get a drink since I forgot to pack anything. Do you want something?"

Instead of answering his question, I ask him the one rattling around in my head. "Are you ashamed to be seen with me?"

His blue eyes open wide, and for a second his mouth drops open. "Why would you think that? Of course, I'm not ashamed to be seen with you."

Then I have a terrible thought. It's because of my age.

"Are you embarrassed because I'm older than you?" I ask, my voice trembling because I'm not sure I want to know the answer to that.

But he laughs and shakes his head. "A whole three or four years? You're twenty-seven, not fifty-seven, Savannah. On top of that, I think I might look older than you, so no, I'm not embarrassed to be seen with you because you're a whopping forty months older than me."

Now I'm embarrassed. Looking down toward the beach towel, I feel my face begin to turn as red as the stripe I'm staring at. "Oh. Then why are you acting like you're so nervous?"

Cash kneels down on the towel and crawls forward until I can't avoid looking into his eyes. They're filled with sincerity, but I don't know what he's going to say to answer my question. I don't know what I want him to say. I guess the truth. If he's not ashamed to be seen with me, why is he acting like he is?

He takes my hands in his and smiles up at me. "I

didn't realize I was acting any way, but I am nervous. I don't want to blow this."

"How could you blow it? All we're doing is hanging out on a towel at the beach."

"I get the feeling you're used to better than this, so I wanted you to be impressed. So far, that's not really going well, unfortunately."

"Better than this?" I ask, completely confused now. "Better as in what?"

A sheepish look settles into his face, and he looks away like he really is embarrassed now. "Better than just hanging out. I thought that this would be fun, but then I realized when we got here that this is pretty low budget for someone like you."

Oh. Now I understand. He's worried I think this isn't classy enough for someone like me. I need to dissuade him from that notion immediately, or we're never going to have a chance together.

"Cash, I'm fine with whatever we do. I don't judge things based on how much they cost. Do you think I do that?"

He looks up at me and tries to smile but doesn't really succeed in making me think he's happy at this moment. "No, not at all, but you can't deny that you're used to nice things. Your husband was able to give you those things. I just worried that you wouldn't be impressed with this."

Now I smile, but it's genuine because he's so sweet. "I am used to nice things, but I don't judge nice by the amount something costs. If that were the case, the eight dollar sodas you're going to buy when you go to that stand would impress me, which they won't. I have the things I want, but what I really want is to spend time with you."

He sighs like my words have taken the weight of the world off his shoulders, and this time when he smiles, it's big and lights up his beautiful blue eyes. "I want to spend time with you too, so good. I'm glad we got that straightened out. You sure you don't want one of those eight dollar sodas since I'm going up there for one for me?"

I lean down to press a kiss onto his lips and shake my head. "No expensive soda for me. I have water."

Cash looks up at me, and all I see is someone I want to spend as much time as possible with from now on. I don't care how we met or what he does for a living. I have enough money that I don't need to worry about any of that. What matters is how he makes me feel, and right now, I feel like the luckiest woman in the world.

When he stands up, he kisses me again, making butterflies flutter in my stomach when his lips touch mine. "I'll be right back. Then we can lay around or go in the water or do whatever you want, okay?"

"Okay."

I watch him walk away across the sand toward the little stand a few hundred yards away and can't stop myself from staring at his legs. The man has great legs. Makes me think I'd love to be doing something else at this moment that doesn't involve sand or sunscreen or anything but the two of us naked in bed.

As I make a mental note to be sure that's how we

end our beach day, I slide my t-shirt up over my head and lean back on my hands to enjoy the feel of the sun on my body. Just a few minutes won't be bad, but as soon as Cash gets back, I'm going to have him slather sunscreen all over me and then I'll do it for him.

I don't want to lose him too.

MY EYES CLOSED, I LIE ON MY STOMACH AND REVEL in the feel of the warmth of the sun and Cash's gentle touch as he rubs sunscreen all over my back. He smooths the lotion over the area where my bikini top is tied, and that's my cue to move my hair and hold it off to the side so he can cover my shoulders.

"This stuff says it's SPF 100. That's got to be equal to you wearing three layers of clothes to the beach," he says in my ear before planting a kiss on my cheek.

"Skin cancer is a terrible thing, Cash. When you're done with me, I'm doing you so you'll be safe too."

"Arms now. I tan, so I don't think I need the one hundred level stuff," he says with a chuckle.

I roll over and sit up to give him my best disappointed look. "Just because you tan doesn't mean you're safe. Your turn. Hand me the bottle and lie on your back."

He hesitates for a moment, but then he relents and does what I want. Folding his arms behind his head, he smiles at me. "I don't mind the part where you rub every inch of my body. It's just that you're rubbing it with thick, white goo. That's not something I like."

With a squirt, I send some of the lotion onto his

chest and begin to smooth it over his skin. "I want you to live a long life, Cash. I'd hate to think I could have made that possible and didn't."

Stopping me, he takes my hands in his and kisses one and then the other. I see sadness in his eyes, but I don't know why.

"I'm sorry, Savannah. I forgot. Feel free to cover me from head to toe."

"Okay. I probably won't do anything with the soles of your feet, and you can be happy that I won't be putting any on the parts covered by your bathing suit," I say as I slide my slippery hands down over his abs to his waist.

"Thank God for small favors."

I lean down and kiss his lips. "I'll save my attention to those parts for later."

He smiles and asks, "The soles of my feet? I had no idea you have a foot fetish."

When he's cute like this, I can't help but giggle. "I don't, but I do like what's under this bathing suit. Have you ever been to a nude beach? I'd love it if this was one."

Cash shakes his head and pursing his lips makes a smacking sound. "No, but now I'm imagining you on a nude beach and I'm thinking I'll all for it. I think I remember hearing about some nudist colony back in Tampa."

"There's one down the coast a bit in Fort Pierce, but the most beautiful one I've ever been to is in Hawaii," I say as I squeeze out more sunscreen and start to rub it on his legs.

I watch his attention move from me to something nearby, so I look in that direction and see a woman with two children staring at us. Her face is twisted into the tightest grimace I've ever seen, and her arms are folded across her chest. I don't need to be an expert in body language to know she's unhappy about something.

But what? She's at the beach, and it's a beautiful day. What could be better than this?

Glancing back at Cash, I shake my head in confusion. "Do you know her? Because I know I don't."

He shrugs and shakes his head too. "Not that I know of. She seems downright miserable, though, considering she's sitting at the beach."

"I know, right? Like what could be so bad that she has to be throwing that scowl around like that?"

Behind me, her children run screaming into the water, and a second later, she gives us the answer for what's bothering her so much today. "You know, this is a family beach. Perhaps you can keep that in mind?"

My mouth drops open in shock, and Cash looks up at me like he can't believe she has a problem with us. What did we do? All we've accomplished since we put our towel down was covering each other in sunscreen.

He gives me a wink and turns his head to the left to look over at her. "Are you saying you have a problem with us not having kids? You know, that's not what family beach means."

His comment upsets her even more, and she angrily points at my hands as they continue to rub lotion into his legs. "That's obscene! There are children around!"

Cash and I exchange looks, unsure what she's talking about. "Protecting against the harmful effects of the sun's rays is obscene?" I ask, still confused what's wrong with this woman.

"Obviously not!" she huffs out. "The way you're rubbing him and he was rubbing you is, though. My children watched the whole thing, for God's sake."

"So your kids watched two people protect their skin against cancer?" Cash asks with more than a hint of edge to his voice now. "Good lord. What will happen to them now? Why don't you pay more attention to the fact that your doughy white skin and your kids' skin is being fried like bacon on a griddle and leave us alone, okay?"

The woman huffs again in disgust and gets herself up on her feet to walk away, leaving her baking kids alone in the water. I watch her for a moment and then look back at him, amazed by that entire interaction.

"You don't think we were being obscene, do you? I was just putting lotion on your skin."

Cash sits up to kiss me sweetly on the lips. "No. I think she's ridiculous, and I'm wondering how she ever got two kids being that uptight."

Hanging my head, I feel like every person on the beach is looking at us now. "Maybe we should just go. I don't really like being out in the sun anyway."

I want to shrink down into the sand and become so small no one notices me. I was only trying to make sure we were safe. That people would think there's something wrong with how we were acting makes me want to disappear.

"Hey, Savannah. Don't listen to her. You and I did nothing wrong. For God's sake, the two of us are wearing more fabric on our body than most people here. She's just a prude."

He lifts my chin with his fingertip and gives me one of his smiles I love. "Don't let her ruin our time, okay?"

As much as I want to believe he's right, I can't help but feel on display now. I hate that. All today was supposed to be was a nice time and now I have to pretend it's still fun while inside I want nothing but to leave.

"I'll try."

"Tell you what. Why don't we go in the water and have some fun. Maybe by the time we get back, she'll have been eaten by a shark and we won't have to bother with her."

I know he's trying to cheer me up by being silly, so I roll my eyes. "A land shark? If we're in the water, won't the shark out there eat us too?"

Cash stands up and takes my hand to pull me up. "I didn't really think that through, but whatever works, I'm good for. Land shark. Regular shark. Just forget about her and let's have a good time."

He tugs me by the arm down to the water and kisses me just before we jump into a wave rolling toward us. It's warm but refreshing, and that episode with that woman begins to fade into the past. I still feel bad about what happened, but something about the way he's trying so hard to make sure we have a good day makes it impossible to stay upset.

A couple nearby makes out like they're about to have sex right there in front of us, and I nudge Cash's shoulder before whispering, "I hope she doesn't see them. She might go blind from the sight of people kissing."

As he looks over at them, he slides his arms around my waist to pull me to his body. In my ear, he says with a chuckle, "I'm pretty sure I'm about to tell them to get a room."

I look up into those beautiful blue eyes of his and smile. "I think that woman's attitude is rubbing off on you. It's not like they're doing anything wrong."

With a laugh, he nods. "You'd think considering what I do myself that public displays of affection wouldn't bother me in the least. I think she is rubbing off on me."

His mention of being as escort catches me by surprise, even though it shouldn't, obviously. Still, it makes me recoil, and I turn out of his hold to swim away.

When he catches up to me a few seconds later, I feel stupid for acting like I am. I know I'm not the only person Cash has ever had a job with. Cheyenne may think I'm a naïve fool, but I'm not that stupid.

"Hey, what happened there?" he asks as he hugs me from behind.

"Nothing. I was just being stupid. Ignore me, please," I say quietly, too embarrassed to face him.

He spins me around so I don't have a choice and

looks into my eyes. I feel so open and vulnerable. I want to look away, but I don't want to make this even worse.

"It's really nothing, Cash. Honest. I was just being stupid."

Shaking his head, he smiles. "No, you weren't. I was being insensitive. I'm so used to my life that I sometimes forget that others aren't."

He stops speaking, and I have a feeling he wants to tell me something. I wait, the water lapping against my skin as I stare up into his eyes, but then it seems to pass.

"Please don't let this ruin our day, Savannah. I want you to have fun. Just know that there's no one but you now, okay?"

The way he says that makes me want so much to believe him. He sounds sincere. Could he be telling the truth, though?

I wrap my arms around his neck and press a kiss onto his wet lips. "Okay. Let's swim for a little bit and then get something to eat. Sound good?"

Cash smiles and kisses me. "That sounds perfect."

CHAPTER TWENTY

S avannah

CASH'S THUMB GENTLY RUBS AGAINST MY forefinger as we drive back home. He's held my hand the entire trip back, even though we haven't said much during the ride. After that horrible woman and her problem with the sunscreen we were putting on and that little awkwardness I created a few minutes after that, we went on to have an incredible day at the beach.

Exhausted, I look over at him in the driver's seat and say quietly, "Thank you for today. It was just what I needed."

He smiles as he switches lanes to pass another car. "I think the next time we should do the nude beach. Just one question. Do people put sunscreen everywhere at a nude beach?"

I watch as his expression morphs into one of genuine concern. He really can be very funny, but I get the sense he isn't trying to joke right now.

"You have to be careful. Can you imagine if *that* got sunburned?" I say with a giggle.

"Oooh, that sounds bad. Strange that in all the time I've had it that it's never gotten to see the sun," he says with a smile. "Do they have special lotion for that part of the body? And what do women do?"

"What do you mean what do women do?" I ask, unsure where he's going with this discussion.

Looking over at me, he explains, "Well, I made the mistake of touching my leg and then rubbing my eye this afternoon, and I felt like my eyeball was on fire. That's just an eye. What happens if you get sunscreen up inside you? I'd have to think that would burn like a son of a bitch."

I lift his hand to my lips to kiss his knuckles. "I think you might be overthinking this a little bit. Maybe we could make sure to have an umbrella for the nude beach trip? That could solve a multitude of problems."

He thinks about it for a few seconds and nods. "Yeah, that could work."

We fall back into a comfortable silence for the next couple minutes. I watch the road signs pass by and look up into the sky as the sun begins to set. It's been a perfect day. I haven't had one of those in a long time.

And it's all because of Cash.

If it weren't for him, I would have never gone to

that beach. Having him by my side gives me the courage to do things I've wanted to for so long.

"Would you like to see my place?" he asks into the silence of the car.

That's the first time he's ever offered to let me see any part of his life. All I've known of him so far is who he is when he's with me at my house.

"Yes, I'd love that," I answer with probably more enthusiasm than he expected.

It's just that letting me into that part of his world says to me that this isn't what Cheyenne claimed it was. I've put that out of my mind for the past few days, even as she's called and texted more than once to make sure to remind me that he's a paid escort so he couldn't actually want to have a relationship with me.

I haven't bothered to tell her that's not true anymore. I haven't paid for anything after the wedding reception. Ever since that Tuesday he stopped over upset about his mother, we haven't been escort and client at all.

Not that I know what we are, except tonight I'm the woman he's taking to his apartment.

"We're almost there. I thought maybe you'd like to see it since I've seen your house a few times."

"I do. I just wonder…"

As soon as the words leave my mouth, I regret them. We had such a great day, and now I've opened up a can of worms because my sister's warnings about him keep replaying on a loop in my head.

Cash looks over at me, his expression serious. God, why do I do things like this?

"What? What's wrong, Savannah?"

I smile and wave it all away. "Nothing. I can't wait to see it."

He turns the car toward the exit, thankfully focused on something other than my stupid slip up. Hopefully, his apartment isn't too far from here, and we can concentrate on that.

A few minutes later after getting through traffic, he pulls into a parking lot in front of what I think must be his building and parks the car. Before I can begin talking about how much I can't wait to see his place, he turns in his seat to face me and I see he hasn't let go of what I said back there on the highway.

"Tell me what you're wondering about. Please. I thought you had a great time today. Didn't you?"

Oh, God. The way he says that, like I'm silently harboring some disappointment over a day he worked to make so fun for both of us, makes me wish I hadn't said those three stupid words.

I can't face him now, so I focus my attention on my hand in my lap even as he holds my other hand and gives it a squeeze. "I had a great time. I swear. Please don't let what I said ruin everything. Just forget I ever said anything, okay?"

He can't let it go, though.

"Tell me what you're wondering, Savannah."

I don't answer, keeping my focus on my lap, so he answers for me. "You're wondering if I truly want to be with you or if none of this is real because it started out with me as an escort and you as a client. That's it, isn't it?"

Tears burn my eyes as I shake my head. "Please don't say anymore. I feel like I already ruined this day."

"Look at me, Savannah. I want to say something to you, so look at me."

Dread like I haven't felt in a long time fills me, but I can't avoid facing him. I slowly turn to see him looking at me, and in his eyes, I swear I see hurt. I have ruined everything. Why couldn't I just enjoy what we were doing together instead of worrying whether or not my sister was right?

"I'm sorry, Cash. I shouldn't have said a word."

A tiny smile lifts the corners of his mouth, giving me some relief. Then he begins to speak, and I'm overcome with emotion.

"I want to be completely honest with you. Yes, we started out with me being paid to take you to that wedding reception, but after that, I haven't been working when we've been together. I like you, Savannah. I like spending time with you. The more we're together, the more I want, to be honest."

"I'm so sorry. I didn't mean to force you to say all of that. My sister said a bunch of things the other day, and I can't seem to get them out of my mind. It's stupid, so I'm sorry."

He leans in and kisses me sweetly, making my heart soar and tears fill my eyes. "You don't have to be sorry. We started out differently than other couples do, but we're the same as everyone else now, don't you think?"

"We're a couple?" I ask, my voice full of hope

that's what he truly means, as I cradle his face and look into those beautiful blue eyes. "Is that what you think?"

He nods and casually shrugs like this is something perfectly commonplace. "Yeah. We like each other, sleep together, and now we've gone on an official date today to the beach. We might have done things in the wrong order, but that sounds like we're a couple to me."

Thrilled at how normal he makes everything seem, I throw my arms around his neck and kiss him. "I think so too. Thank you!"

Leaning back, he asks, "For what?"

"I don't know. For not making me feel stupid for wondering."

He gives me a soft kiss and sighs against my lips. "Now when we go to my place, try to keep your expectations low. I'd hate for my apartment to ruin this day."

"Oh, you don't have to worry. I'm sure it'll be great."

I'm just glad I didn't ruin this day with my questions.

"Then let's go up and we can have a drink after that drive," he says while he turns off the car.

Lost in my happiness at what's just happened between Cash and me, I don't see the two men standing just outside the car on Cash's side until one of them taps on the window. Instantly frightened, I clamp my hand onto his forearm to stop him from leaving the car to talk to them.

He doesn't seem worried, though, and opens the door. "Yes?"

I watch in fear that they're going to jump him, but before my eyes, something even worse happens. The two men introduce themselves as Gainesville police officers and the next thing I know, they're telling him he's under arrest and spinning him around to put handcuffs on him!

"What are you doing? Why are you doing this?" I ask frantically as I hurry to get out of the car.

By the time I get to where the three of them stand, Cash has his hands behind his back in cuffs and they're forcing him to go with them in their car. I don't know what to do or what to say to them to make them release him.

"Cash, what's happening? Why are they doing this?" I ask in tears.

The last thing I see before they put him into the back seat of the police car is his face. He looks sad and frightened, but just as they're about to take him away, he smiles.

"Go home and stay safe. I'll be fine. Don't worry."

I open my mouth to ask him to tell me what's going on, but my chance passes by and the cop slams the car door with Cash in the back seat. As tears roll down my cheeks, I watch as the car drives away, leaving me standing there alone and confused about what just happened.

Unsure what to do, I call the only person I know who might understand. Cheyenne answers quickly, giving me a tiny sense of relief when I hear her say sweetly, "Savannah, I was just thinking about you."

Before she can say another word, I blurt out, "Cash was just taken away in handcuffs by the Gainesville police. I'm standing here in the parking lot in front of his apartment building and they just drove away with him."

"Oh, honey, I heard rumors that the service was being watched in the past week, but I thought you stopped talking to him. Savannah, he's been nabbed for being an escort. They're going to charge him with prostitution, along with a bunch of other things."

I don't hear anything after that. She continues to talk, and I tell her where I am, but my mind is numb from the news that Cash has been arrested for exactly what he did for me when he acted as my date for my brother's wedding reception.

The man I'm in love with arrested for the very thing that brought him into my life. Oh, God! I can't let him stay in jail for that.

I have to help him.

LOOK FOR AMBITIOUS, THE CONCLUSION TO CASH AND SAVANNAH'S STORY!

ABOUT THE AUTHOR

K.M. Scott writes contemporary romance stories of sexy, intense, and unforgettable love. A New York Times and USA Today bestselling author, she's been in love with romance since reading her first romance novel in junior high (she was a very curious girl!). Under her Gabrielle Bisset name, she write paranormal and historical romance. She lives in Pennsylvania with a herd of animals and when she's not writing can be found reading or feeding her TV addiction.

Be sure to visit K.M.'s Facebook page at **https://www.facebook.com/kmscottauthor** for all the latest on her books, along with giveaways and other goodies! And to hear all the news on K.M. Scott books first, sign up for her newsletter today and be sure to visit her website at **http://www.kmscottbooks.com**

Notorious (NeXt #1)

Infamous (NeXt #2)

Ravenous (NeXt #3)

Ambitious (NeXt #4)

If I Dream (Corrupted Love #1)

If You Fight (Corrupted Love #2)

If We Fall (Corrupted Love #3)

Corrupted Love Trilogy Box Set

Crave (Addicted To You #1)

Adore (Addicted To You #2)

Shatter (Addicted To You #3)

Claim (Addicted To You #4)

Addicted To You Series Box Set

In The Darkness (Project Artemis #1)

After The Storm (Project Artemis #2)

Behind The Scenes (Project Artemis #3)

Project Artemis Box Set

Hard Work (Finding The One #1)

Big Love (Finding The One #2)

Sweet Things

Private Secretary

K.M.'S BOOKS ARE IN AUDIOBOOK TOO!

www.ingramcontent.com/pod-product-compliance
Lightning Source LLC
Chambersburg PA
CBHW020113180626
46812CB00006B/2575